SHADOW'S ANGEL

Shadow's Angel

Leesa Ellen

I am the sun when it rises and sheds
its heat,
I am the cool sea water that laps at
your feet.
I am the moon when it lights a way
through the dark,
and the feeling of love that embraces
your heart.

*

For Granny Borowski, who woke an
angel.

Some helpful Aussie terms.

Ute: Similar to an American-style Pickup, but different. A favourite type of car for many Aussies.

Bugger: A) A statement similar to Damn! or Bollocks!

           B) You little bugger - You naughty little thing.

Snags/Bangers: Sausages

Bloody: A) Bloody hell! - Oh wow!

          B) That's bloody gold - That's awesome!

          C) Bloody rain! - Damn rain!

          D) It's bloody cold! - It's really cold!

She'll be right: Everything will be ok.

You reckon?: Do you think so?

1

Crash

It feels like an eternity since I looked up from my phone and realised I'd driven straight through a red light. In reality, it hasn't even been a few seconds. Not enough time to react. No chance of swerving. So I'm sitting here, frozen to stone, white knuckles clenching the wheel, eyes unable to tear themselves from the giant truck tires only inches away from flattening my car.

For the moment, it seems like the tires have stopped moving. Everything has. As though I'm politely being given the space I need to recap the things that have happened in my life up to this point.

All the shaping moments are there: my first day at school. Meeting my, now best friend Astrid, at horse riding camp. Mum and Dad's divorce. Dad's move to London for work last year.

The moments flick past like a formality, as if they want to make sure that before I die I fully appreciate the life I'm leaving behind. Shadow is there in almost all of them: In my arms with his sharp puppy teeth caught in my hair and his pointed cattle dog ear tickling my nose. Licking my tears after Astrid and her family moved three thousand kilometres away to Victoria two years ago. Buckled in beside me on my first solo trip around the block as a licensed driver. I don't need any reminding to appreciate him, and as time slips forward a fraction of a second, dragging the tires with it until they're touching the side of my car, he's the one thing that stays on my mind.

Impact. Hard, as though I've been hit by a freight train. I feel my upper body skew then the grip of my seatbelt.

Everything stops again.

The picture through my passenger window is now the undercarriage of the truck. I can see all the way back to the last wheels on its trailer. There's eighteen all up. I wonder how many of them will roll over me before the driver can stop. The darkness between them is like a black hole sucking me into the next moment of my life. I wish I didn't have to relive this one, or those bound to follow. I need hope, not a kick-me-while-I'm-down reminder of the ignorance that led me to where I am now. But that's exactly what I'm about to get: the twenty-twenty vision clarity of hindsight. It's this morning.

I'm waking up at the beach house that Mum and her boyfriend, Robert, bought a few years back. The sunlight pouring through the window is making my legs burn, it's going to be another sweltering hot North Queensland day. It's Shadow's and my first time here alone and I'm too excited to sleep in. Eighteen today, and for the first time in just over two years, I'll get to see Astrid again. Her plane's due in at the Cairns airport at nine-fifteen and we've got a whole week together to do whatever we want.

Shadow's sharing my pillow. His nose is so close it's blowing little snot bubbles into my hair. He's got one front leg stretched across my neck and he's staring at me like some creepy stalker who's been watching me sleep all night.

I'm reaching for my phone to see what the time is, but it's not where I left it on the bedside table. The wattle-yellow summer dress Mum gave me isn't where I left it either. It *was* hanging over the end of the bed. I'm thinking it's probably just fallen on the floor and hoping it's not too wrinkled. It's the only one I really like because the lining fluffs the skirt out a little bit, making me at least look like I have hips.

The flashbacks jump ahead to where I've just found my phone out on the back sundeck in Shadow's food bowl. It's eight-thirty already! I thought I was up early because I didn't hear the alarm. Now I know why. I don't know why he took it though. He's following me with the same stalker eyes I woke up to. Creeping along behind like he knows he's been naughty.

There's the dress! I'm asking Shadow, "Why is it under the spare bed? And why aren't my car keys on the coffee table anymore?"

The keys are under the wet towel I dropped on the bathroom floor last night. He's tried to hide them for some reason. He must know I can't take him with me to pick Astrid up.

Now I'm hugging him while he sits sulking beside the car. I'm telling him the air conditioning isn't working and I can't leave him in this January heat while we go to the mall. He's making me uneasy: all the thefts, the crazy eyes, the sulking.

He's tugging at my dress as I get out of the car to shut the gate behind me. I'm promising him it'll only be a couple of hours and trying to pry my dress from between his teeth without tearing it. I'm feeling even more uneasy now. He's never acted like this before, never been so determined to stop me from leaving.

There are goosebumps on my arms as I drive away. The car's temperature gauge reads thirty-two degrees. The goosebumps don't belong there.

I can hear a dog howling. It sounds mournful, anxious, miserable. It sounds...like Shadow.

I'm running so late that I didn't even put shoes on or brush my hair. There's a pair of old flats in the back. I'll just have to throw them on when I get there.

I'm wondering why Shadow is howling. Stop looking in the rear-view mirror, I'm telling myself. He'll be fine. It's just a few hours.

I hear the text message beep from my phone. Don't pick it up, I warn myself. Wait until after the intersection. But I know it'll be Astrid. She will have landed by now and she'll be wondering where I am.

I can't stop myself. Be there soon, I'm replying. But I won't be, because the flashbacks have caught up to reality, I've just driven straight through a red light, and the truck's wheels have started turning again.

There's a sense of glee about them as they plough into the side of my car. The buckling metal and smashing glass create the perfect soundtrack for their sadistic intentions: it feels like they've been looking forward to this bit.

One climbs up over the bonnet, the other crashes through

the back-passenger window before venturing further up onto the roof, looking to do as much damage as possible.

I feel the crush of every bone in my body and taste the blood in my mouth. I should scream, fight for consciousness, at least remember to keep breathing, but all I can think of is Shadow. Can he hear what's happening? I'm not even a kilometre away. Is he still howling? I can't leave him. Mum doesn't like him, her boyfriend Robert's allergic to him, Dad's in England, Astrid's perfect, but she's only up here for a week, after that he'll be completely alone.

Silence falls around me. I wonder how many wheels made it over my car. I can't see the sun; I must be under the trailer. There's another black hole forming in the darkness. I can feel it sucking me in again and I can't begin to imagine what might be on the other side.

Pitch black, weightlessness, light, calm…, Shadow?

He's waiting behind the gate where I pried my yellow dress from between his teeth only moments ago. He's not howling anymore, just sitting as still as a statue of a lost soul, ears pricked toward the sound of a lonely future.

"You knew," I say. "You tried to stop me from leaving."

The serenity of the moment begs me to lie down. This must be heaven. I pat my chest for Shadow to rest his head on, but when he does his weight pushes down on my lungs until it becomes impossible to draw in even the slightest sliver of air.

I can't move him aside, there's no strength in my arms. "Shadow, what's happening?"

He locks his eyes onto mine, as if to draw my attention away from not only the weight but the pain building beneath it. His mouth begins to move but it's not Shadow's mouth alone, more like a blurry morphing of his and a human mouth.

"Stay with me." I hear him say, in a voice suited more to an adult man.

The blur worsens. I can't find Shadow's mouth anymore, or his eyes. I can't even make out the sandy-coloured heart-shaped mask around them. My eyelids hang heavier and heavier until no amount of effort will keep them open. Just for a second, I think.

One second becomes two, two become three, then..., "STAY WITH ME."

It's the same voice, but it's not Shadow. My eyes are open again, my vision almost gone. I'm back in my car together with every inch of unfathomable agony. There's a man out-side my smashed window. He has Shadow's voice.

I try to focus on him, but my eyes have given up. They want to close. I grant them their wish and there in the dark-ness, once again, is Shadow - and the calm.

"I'm dying, Shadow," I say. "I can't take care of you any-more. You need to go to Astrid."

I don't know whether I spoke the words out loud or only thought them, but as Shadow begins to howl again, I know they were my last.

That was the day I died.

2

A-Wake

Shadow lies splayed out on the front veranda's cool wooden floorboards, not far from the gate where I said goodbye to him almost a week ago. His silky anchor-grey coat is stifled in shine by a layer of the same salty sea air that builds up on the beach house's windows over time, and without lifting his head, his eyes, equally as dull in shine, follow the wishful pricking of his ears every time they hear my name.

The same jogger he plucked from my unpacked suitcase, my left one, always his favourite for some reason, is squashed under his chin pushing the corners of his mouth around into an especially human-like frown. He brought the jogger outside along with my pyjama shorts, one of my skirts and my favourite crop top, and positioned them like a barricade around his body. It's his way of telling the mourners who sombrely clutter the living room and outside areas of the house that he prefers to grieve alone for the moment.

He doesn't know it, but I'm sitting right beside him, listening to the sounds of teaspoons clinking and subdued conversations. Even the footsteps from the visitors are restrained as they cross the polished timber floor, as though anything more than a tiptoe would be a sign of disrespect.

It's the strangest thing to be here, completely unseen, watching my family, neighbours, and respectfully enough, a bunch of the girls from school neither Astrid nor I ever bothered to get close to.

Maybe Mum's boyfriend Robert asked the girls to come, for my parents' sake. I suppose nobody wants to find out their daughter only had two friends. It never bothered me though. I had Astrid and Shadow. That was all I ever needed.

I've been here with Shadow since the day of my accident, existing in a strange state, void of all senses except for one – a kind of 'nothing' that feels like it should be something, but isn't.

It's much the same as the stitches I received in my leg a few years ago after falling from my bike while riding home from school. The nurse gave me a local anaesthetic and I remember watching the tiny, hooked needle pierce my skin. I panicked over the thought of the imminent pain, but felt nothing. I watched right to the end, cringing with anticipation, expecting each new stab to be the one when the anaesthetic would wear off and the pain would be there. It didn't wear off and there wasn't any pain. I felt nothing.

That's how this feels, like a physical nothing.

My appearance is another oddity; I look exactly as I did *before* the crash. There's no blood, no broken bones, my wattle-yellow dress is unmarked, my feet bare, and my curly, blonde hair? Well, I'd like to say as neat as ever, but as tangled as ever suits better.

On that first day, I don't remember leaving the wreckage or how I made it back home. I just found myself sitting next to Shadow again, behind our gate, listening to the distant sound of sirens. It was confusing. I couldn't figure out how I could have walked away from the crash unscathed. It had to be a miracle. Then I tried to give Shadow a hug and the hope of a miracle shattered into a million pieces; my arms drifted straight through his body. That was the first worst moment of my death and the first time I felt the 'nothing'.

I sat there with him until sometime around midday when a police car pulled up and I saw Astrid in the back seat. She looked pale enough to take my place as the ghost in this story and her dark chocolate hair had lightened to a mousey brown since the last time I saw her. I'd like to think her insomniac appearance was nothing more than the result of the vitamin-D deficiency she complained about; a common thing for sun-deprived Victorians. *That* could have at least been easily fixed by a good soak in the North Queensland sun.

The police car had driven her in from the other end of the street, presumably so as not to expose her to the sight of the scene which by the sound of tow truck winches and re-verse beepers was still being cleared. The uniformed driver then steadied her violent shaking as she stumbled out of the car, and almost had to lift her legs for her as he escorted her through the gate.

For a brief moment she'd lifted her grass-green eyes to-ward the intersection and I'd caught the torment in them; a myriad of emotions that flickered between utter disbelief, ag-onising devastation, and total shock.

That was the second worst moment.

Later that afternoon, Mum had made it to the house – the third worst moment. Two days after that, Dad and his new girlfriend Carol flew in – the fourth.

From there on I've been a completely aimless, silent observer. I've listened to all the funeral organising phone calls and even saw my own coffin as it was lowered into the ground beneath a dark copper, granite headstone. 'Our Darling Lucinda. Gone much too soon' were the words inscribed, and the 'too soon' part couldn't have been more accurate.

Throughout everything, though, I've felt only the 'nothing'. Now, sitting with Shadow on the front veranda watching the proceedings of my own wake, I am beginning to wonder – why am I even here?

***

I can see Mum through the window. Understandably numb, she hasn't spoken a word all day, just stared blankly at random objects, like the small, framed picture she now holds in her hands. It's of Shadow and I on the beach at sunset.

It was taken only a few weeks ago, just after graduation. I'm wrapped in a beach towel, standing with my arms spread out like the world is my oyster, and Shadow's jumping up trying to reach the stick I'm holding.

I know she's vividly reliving that day again; I can see the pride flickering in her clear blue eyes. I think it was one of the only times she was honestly proud of me, most of the time I'm sure she saw me as more of an annoyance. There's something else there as she focuses on Shadow's image. Pity? Anxiety? I guess she's wondering what she's supposed to do with him now that I'm gone.

I imagine she'll be planning to keep Shadow: not because she loves him, but because, as my mother, it's what she's expected to do. Eventually though, her feeling of obligation will pass and she'll be stuck with a dog she never really wanted.

Dad would also take Shadow if he were still living here in Australia. I can't see him wanting to spend the money to have Shadow flown over to England though, which is fair enough considering they didn't know each other long enough to form any kind of connection.

Mum's finally torn herself away from my picture. She's spotted Dad by the kitchen and has managed her first words for the day. "Where's Shadow? Can you bring him in, please?"

I don't know how much luck he'll have. There are only two people in the world Shadow listens to, and since he doesn't realise I'm still here with him, he's grabbed my jogger and taken off to find option number two. The person we should be walking along the beach with right now – Astrid.

Leaving the bulk of the mourners, I follow Shadow down around the side of the house and up on to the back sundeck. It's here we find Astrid curled into one side of Mum's cane outdoor two-seater with her hair draped over one shoulder and knees tucked up under the black wraparound dress she bought yesterday. She had to pin the V-neck all the way up to her collar bone after Mum told her that boobs had no place at a funeral. Even on good days the two never could find a compliment for each other.

On any other day, the distant MacAlistar Range and the setting sun behind her would make a spectacularly serene backdrop. Today it just highlights Astrid's loneliness. She looks like she's trapped in an oil painting, the kind you can't stop looking at because it's so beautiful yet sad at the same time. She looks completely lost and Shadow's noticed it too.

Wanting to get as close as possible with as little disturbance as possible, he eases himself up and squishes into the space beside her. Still clutching my jogger between his teeth, he tucks all four paws in tight and sinks his head into her lap.

I have to laugh at him, and at how much my jogger must stink. "No, not at all disturbing," I tease. He doesn't hear me, of course. It's something I'm still struggling to get used to.

Unable to resist the troubled groan Shadow lets out, Astrid turns away from the sun, cups her arm around him and pulls him in even closer. His desperate hold on my jogger triggers a stream of tears and a tremble in her voice, "You won't be letting her go anytime soon either, huh?"

Shadow groans again, Astrid goes back to staring into space, and the afternoon falls silent.

I watch Shadow and Astrid until the lush greens of the range lose the sun and turn the colour of a washed-up old wine bottle. Somebody switches the inside and sundeck lights on, and in packs of two and three, the mourners start to make their way to their cars out on the street. Mum's still sitting inside, staring blankly at my photo again, and Dad's found a beer and a Fijian cane barstool on the front veranda.

This was supposed to be a holiday for Astrid, our chance to finally spend some time together after over two years apart. Instead she is curled up with Shadow, mourning the loss of the only person in this house who really ever cared about either of them. Neither she, Shadow, Mum, Dad, nor anyone knows I am here, and why should they? After all, how often does a dead person attend their own funeral?

3

Argument

As I suspected, Mum's insisting on keeping Shadow. Robert's trying to convince her otherwise. "You've got all of Lucinda's stuff at home, darling. Think of her dad. He's got nothing except a couple of photos. Maybe he'd like to take the dog back home with him."

Dad's overheard from his seat on the front veranda and halted midway through a sip of his beer. He's squinting at Carol, who's hiding from Mum behind the outer wall of the house and dramatically miming 'we can't. It's too expensive!'

Mum's grasping at straws. "I know what you're thinking, Robert. I know I've never given two hoots about him before, but he's my daughters' dog. He's all I've got left of her."

She's started sobbing. "You don't think I'm capable of looking after a dog, do you?"

"That's not what I meant!" Robert lies, and quite badly too.

Mum dabs at her eyeliner with an already black-stained tissue. A few deep breaths brings her back to the stern-faced woman I grew up with. "Obviously you don't think I can handle it," she pounces on Robert. I feel sorry for him, having myself been at the receiving end of Mum's 'obviously' accusations more times than I can count: obviously you don't think I see the dog hair on the couch; obviously I'm just a silly old woman because I don't want you falling off one of Astrid's horses and breaking your neck.

Robert doesn't get a word in before Mum makes a decision that has me wishing I could feel the walls so I could hit my head against one of them: "I'm going to take him and stay with my friend Claire at Babinda for a while. She said she would be there for me if I needed anything, and I need *this.*"

Claire – a condescendingly proud, lifelong singleton whose reptilian hands wouldn't know how to pat a dog – is so set in her ways it's impossible to imagine she'd allow such a disruption to her routine. I had Shadow with me twice when I begrudgingly accompanied Mum on her visits. Both times, her mere presence made him so nervous that he wouldn't go within ten metres of her.

Whether I like the idea or not makes no difference though. I don't have the voice to change it. If I did, I would push for the best possible outcome for Shadow, the only intelligent solution, the one I now wish I would have thought to plan for. I would tell them to let Shadow go home with Astrid. She's the only one who loves him as much as I do.

***

At breakfast the next morning, Dad and Carol announce they'll be flying back to London straight away. I knew spending too much time here would be more than Dad could handle; I knew he'd want to put as much distance between himself and the centre point of his grief as soon as possible.

I watch them carry their bags out into the early morning sun and I wave - unseen - as the taxi drives them away. Returning to the kitchen, I find Astrid and Mum forlornly milling around the idea of eating something.

Robert's taken a cup of coffee out onto the back sundeck and Shadow has, as usual, practically attached himself to Astrid's legs. He's watching the toaster with only slightly more enthusiasm.

Handing Mum a plate of toast and Vegemite, Astrid nods toward Shadow, "Are you sure he wouldn't be happier coming with me? He'd love it at home. I've already spoken to my parents and, under the circumstances, they said it's fine. We've got heaps of room and I'd really love to have him. Also..." she adds cautiously, "I think, maybe...it's what Lucy might have wanted."

Having only ever seen Astrid as the nuisance friend who talked her daughter out of deportment school and into all things dirt, before finally – thank God – moving away, Mum instantly glows red at the suggestion. Her plate slams with a clang onto the stone-topped kitchen bench, her toast bounces off the edge and slaps Vegemite side down against the floor.

Given a different situation, the fierce contempt with which she then meets Astrid's eyes would be enough to demand silence, but although sharply taken aback, I know my friend understands the implications of Mum's illogical plans for Shadow and I can't blame her one bit for pushing on through the boundaries of respect.

"I jog every morning," she keeps trying, picking up the

plate to occupy her now nervously fidgeting hands. "He's a cattle dog; he needs that exercise. Plus, he's allowed inside!"

She holds Mum's gaze with shaky confidence. "I really don't mean to be rude, but it just makes more sense for him to——"

"He'll be fine," Mum cuts in, her tone an uncompromising warning that reaches Astrid loud and clear.

The room falls into silence, allowing Astrid time to unlock her eyes from Mum's and submissively seek out the floor. "I'm sorry." She turns, as if to put the plate in the sink, then deciding the issue too important to heed Mum's warning, turns back with plate still in hand. Erring once more on the side of caution, she starts again, albeit this time keeping her head low. "If anything happens, though, or you change your mind, please let me know and I'll come straight back up and get him. I really don't want to push you, but you've got to admit he'd be better——"

Mum doesn't let her finish. With a roar loud enough to make the neighbours sit up straight she shocks the plate out of Astrid's hands and has Robert, who I can see through the back glass door, spilling his coffee all over his pants. "THAT'S ENOUGH!"

The plate shatters beside the toast. Its demise ignored by all except for Shadow who, never one to appreciate yelling, ties his imaginary knot around Astrid's legs even tighter until he's almost climbing on top of her feet.

Mum's next words are amplified even more by a rib-bruising finger-to-chest point and the fierce hunt for Astrid's downturned eyes. "MY DAUGHTER...MY DOG! GOT IT?"

When Astrid finally dares to look up, the submission I expected to still see shrouding her face is gone and she glares at Mum with blunt defiance. "You're making a mistake!"

Trembling on the brink of her boiling point and lost for any form of rational argument, Mum stomps from the kitchen, through the living room, and toward the front sliding-glass door. She almost pulls the door off its rails jerking it open with a bang against the stopper. Turning back to Astrid, she calls her out of the kitchen by way of one arm raised in the direction on the street. There's fire, a twisted sense of revenge and five years worth of hatred in her voice when she finally speaks again.

"Don't you have a plane to catch?"

4

Claire's

It's been a month since Mum, Shadow and I came to stay with Claire. About a week ago, Mum started to talk about moving back to Cairns, but she seems to be realising Robert was right: maybe keeping Shadow wasn't such a good idea.

Claire has been reasonably welcoming. She's done everything she can to help Mum, but for the most part, she ignores Shadow. She hasn't been mean to him in any way though, just...non-caring.

As usual, Shadow's on edge around her. There's still no trust. Seeing Mum as the lesser of two evils, he sticks close to her side when Claire's around and the one time she actually acknowledged him by name, he stiffened like a board. I can't imagine she'd ever hurt him, but she clearly doesn't see him as anything more than Mum's baggage. Baggage Mum also seems to be growing tired of lugging around.

I've been by Shadow's side the entire time. I can't feel him any more than he can me, but I've slept beside him every night and walked with him every time he's ventured into the yard to occupy himself with a new smell. Although he's right beside me, I miss him. I miss not being able to hug him and see the joy ripple through his whole body when he squeezes into my arms. Most of all, I miss the wag of his tail. He hasn't wagged it since the last time I could touch him, right before I left for the airport that day.

I wonder how long I'm supposed to stay here; aimlessly following Shadow around, consumed by this 'nothing' feeling. Every day I try to do something that might give me some connection to the living. I try touching objects: a chair, a door, a wall. My hand passes through all of them without the slightest sensation. I try focusing every thought and every molecule of energy on the object, but still nothing.

The most I've tried, though, has been with Shadow. I'd like to believe there's some sense of feeling in my hand when I place it over his back or between his ears. I wish I could will it to be there. Even if it's not the softness I remember, I wouldn't care. Anything, any sensation would be better than the 'nothing'.

***

Five weeks and two days ago, Mum moved into Claire's house and already she's moving out again. Coming to terms with the deepest phase of her grief meant (as predicted) that her feelings of obligation toward a dog she never really wanted are fading.

I had no more choice than Shadow to be anything but a silent listener to Mum and Claire's plans for his future, and although I didn't immediately pick up on it, from the minute I heard how they planned to tackle the situation I began to feel a twinge of 'something'. I'm not sure what it is. It's not so much an actual *feeling*, more like the presence of one. It's like the void is less empty; the 'nothing' is less...nothing. I can't understand it, but I know whatever is causing it is doing so because something about the situation isn't right.

Although they briefly discussed giving Shadow to Astrid, Mum was still too busy calling her an 'insolent child' to properly entertain the idea. Claire dutifully offered to let him stay until Mum figured things out. I could hear the regret soaking through each word as she spoke it, but Mum, too lost for another idea, accepted the offer before Claire could change her mind. So, it was decided and Shadow was doomed. He was staying with Claire the dragon lady.

I understood how they could think it was the smartest option for now, but I couldn't, and still can't understand how they don't realise what this will mean for Shadow. Their idea shows no consideration for him at all, but they've made their decision. So, as Shadow and I stand on the driveway, just past where the last veranda step meets the gravel, Mum shifts her clean, white sedan into gear and calls to Shadow through the open window, "I'll see you next weekend, boy."

The 'nothing' shifts a little further toward 'something', and for some reason I can't help but think this could be the last time Shadow and I ever see Mum again.

***

I can still hear the fading hum of Mum's engine and already Claire has begun to clean up any trace that she was ever anything but alone in the house.

Before Shadow and I even make it back up to the top step, the sliding glass door that leads to the veranda is all but slammed shut. Through it, we watch her drag out the vacuum cleaner and hear her groan at the sight of dog hair-covered furniture. There's no denying it now. With Mum gone, Claire is slipping straight back into her tidy, structured lifestyle, a lifestyle in which a hair-shedding, rotten-meat-eating, mud-puddle loving, overactive cattle dog was never going to fit.

I know that as long as Shadow stays here, his days and nights will be spent alone, either on the veranda or in the yard. Even if my premonition about never seeing Mum again is wrong and she does come back to visit on the weekends, those days will be too far apart to be of any consolation and it won't be long before the visits will become nothing more than a bothersome duty. Sadly, despite any promises she may have made, I don't hold much faith in Mum's dedication to Shadow. He's only here because of her jealousy, spite, and pride. These things won't be nearly reason enough for her to keep coming back.

5

Jogger

The only remnant Shadow has of a happier past is my left jogger. He hasn't let it out of his sight since first grabbing hold of it more than two months ago, and Claire is crazy to think he might let go of it now.

For as long as Shadow's been carrying my jogger around, Claire hasn't given a second thought to it, nor cared to realise what it means to him. How she could overlook it sitting next to his food bowl, while he eats his staple diet of cheap supermarket brand biscuits, is beyond me. How she could not feel even a tinge of empathy seeing it float in his water bowl while he drinks around it, I'll never understand. Somehow though, that's exactly what she's managed to do – until now.

Maybe she thinks that since Mum hasn't visited for two weeks, it's time Shadow also moved on, or maybe it has something to do with the small, rotten, maggot-covered bone he dug up this morning and put into the shoe. He wanted to be able to carry both at the same time.

As disgusting as it sounds, I'd give anything to be able to smell the putrid odour of that bone, to be able to understand exactly why it's driving Shadow and Claire two very different kinds of crazy.

Claire looks sceptical about touching the jogger. Aside from the rotting bone and maggots, the shoe itself these days isn't something any normal person would want to grab hold of without a pair of tongs. After a daily dunking in his food and water bowls, Shadow's had it with him in every puddle of mud he's ever found, in every patch of prickles he's got stuck in, and at every leg-lift stop he's ever made. The once-white fabric is now all different shades of brown and the tongue in-sert flaps loosely between frayed laces.

It's sitting on the veranda. Shadow's holding the toe down with his paw and shoving his nose in under the tongue to pull out the rotting bone.

As Claire watches, her face turns to utter disgust. Even more so as Shadow deviates from the bone and plucks out a couple of maggots that fell off it and back into the jogger. One of the maggots manages to escape. For a second, Shadow can't decide whether to go after it before it disappears through the floorboards or to tuck back into his meal in a shoe.

Luck is on the maggot's side, but before Shadow can get his nose all the way back under the tongue-insert, Claire does something stupid. She reaches in to take my jogger away.

Completely forgetting about the meal within, Shadow quickly snatches my jogger between his teeth and I hear something that raises even my eyebrows – a low, possessive, 'leave my shoe alone' growl.

Claire's heard it too, and in one swift stroke her hand is back by her side. For a moment, she pauses, uncertain of what to do next, then dismisses her doubts by telling herself, "It's just Shadow; he wouldn't hurt a fly." She leans toward my jogger again, albeit with a hint of caution, which she tries, but fails to hide.

Shadow growls again. It's a little higher pitched, sounding more like a plea than a threat, and it instantly gives Claire the confidence boost she needs.

She reaches further, and with a scoffing click of her tongue, says, "Oh, you stupid dog. Get over it. It's just a shoe, for Christ's sake." As her fingers touch my jogger's heel though, Shadow proves to her that it's worth so much more.

He tries as hard as he can to get a firmer grip before Claire can reef it out of his mouth altogether. He snaps his teeth around it twice, each time closer to Claire's hand than the last.

Realising she could possibly get hurt if Shadow tries for a third bite, I want to scream at her to let go, but I'm too late because Shadow's teeth have already snapped all the way up to the heel and have accidentally caught Claire's knuckles in the process.

She lets out a cry halfway between an angry 'what?' and a painful 'ouch!', it comes out as a "Wouch!" At the same time, she quickly draws her hand back to inspect the damage. I can see a slight trickle of blood seeping from her index finger and a shallow puncture wound above the middle knuckle, but the rest appears untouched.

Still holding her wounded hand, Claire stares too disbelievingly at Shadow to scold him. Shadow also appears overwhelmed. Even though it wasn't his fault, he guiltily snatches my jogger from the floor and retreats with his tail between his legs to the far end of the veranda.

I wonder what Claire will decide to do next. I watch her

take a hesitant step toward Shadow and then pause again. He doesn't react, so she takes another step, and another, until the distance between them is no more than a couple of feet. Although obviously wary of Shadow's reaction, she's not about to dishonour her pride, even though it's driving her to do something she knows she probably shouldn't.

With a rush of confidence, she takes a longer and more imposing step, swoops down, yanks my jogger out of Shadow's mouth, then enraged by fear, brandishes it over him as if she's about to hit him with it.

Shadow ducks and squeezes himself as tight as he can into the corner.

Claire seems to enjoy his reaction. "Who's scared now, huh?" she spits.

She turns to walk away, talking to herself as she goes. "What a stupid dog."

Shadow dares to lift his head enough to lock his eyes on my jogger. It's the one keepsake he has from our lives together and he's not prepared to let it go that easily. He springs to his feet and dashes across the veranda in an attempt to retrieve it.

There's no doubt in my mind that should Shadow accidentally get hold of Claire instead of my shoe again, she could end up with a painful sight more than a slight trickle of blood and a shallow puncture wound.

He's less than a stride away and ready to leap.

Claire hears him coming. She turns, freezes for a second, then at the same time as Shadow lifts off, she stashes the jogger behind her back, putting herself directly in Shadow's line of fire.

This isn't going to end well for anyone.

While I know Shadow can't hear me and I know I can't stop him, years of speaking to him has embedded the habit so deep in my subconscious that not even I can stop myself from screaming out, "SHADOW, NO!"

The words have barely left my mouth when Shadow's ears prick. His eyes widen until the whites are showing and he stops dead.

Likely believing Shadow's fury was aimed at her, Claire wastes no time deciding on a reaction. She spins on her heels while she has the chance, drops the jogger, and hightails along the veranda. Not daring to even glance behind, in case Shadow might think to hunt more than the shoe, she gathers enough pace by the time she reaches the steps to take all three in one dramatic leap.

Kicking miniature fairy garden stones up as she goes, she sprints like a panicked gazelle to her car. She almost rips the door off before throwing herself inside, and without a second to lose, slams the door shut with a bang behind her.

I can see her tucked in the driver's seat, clutching the steering wheel while sucking in deep breaths of air, and I can hear her ranting through the slightly cracked window. "You're a dangerous dog, Shadow. When I get back, you're going to the pound. I'll have you put down for this."

I hear the engine turn over and watch Claire's wheels spin small ruts into the gravel before her car bunny-hops into motion. I have no idea where she's going, I doubt even she knows, but as soon as the sound of her motor fades down the street and the afternoon is quiet again, I turn back to Shadow with far more important things on my mind. I think he heard me.

6

Shadow?

Shadow's lying with his head resting on my jogger and an all-too-familiar look of loneliness in his eyes.

My mind flashes back to the moment he was about to leap on Claire. Was it coincidence? Is it possible? If there's a chance something has shifted, if my state of 'nothing' has begun to dissolve, I need to know – and I need to know now before Claire comes back.

As quickly as I can, I bring myself down to Shadow's eye level. I see a heartbreaking sadness. the kind that follows when one dares to hope and then gets let down. It's worse than the look of no hope at all, but it proves he heard me. He must have. Now how do I make him hear me again?

"Shadow?" I try, quietly at first in case it should be so simple. "Shadow? Can you hear me?"

Shadow remains oblivious, decidedly alone, staring through me into the distance.

"Shadow?" I try again, a little louder and moving closer. He blinks, but it doesn't seem to have anything to do with the sound of my voice. I hear a car out on the street. Please don't let that be Claire. It sounds like it turns into the drive-way next door. I can't see it through the tall, wooden fence, but it doesn't matter; it's not coming here. I still have time.

"Shadow! Please!" I beg, as if he's just a stubborn child ignoring his mum. "Please hear me."

Shadow hears nothing.

I don't want to allow them in, but thoughts of Claire returning slip into my mind. I don't know how she plans to catch him after what just happened. I doubt he'll ever let her near him again. Maybe she's gone into town to buy treats to coerce him with. She might be on her way to the pound to ask someone to follow her back with one of those dog-catching nooses. Regardless of what she has planned, the fences surrounding her yard are too high for him to escape over. However she intends to catch him, I have no doubt she'll succeed, which leads to even worse thoughts: thoughts of what she'll do with him when she does. Thoughts of Shadow in a cage at the pound. Shadow lying lifeless on a steel table after they've stuck the needle in his front leg. Shadow's body being thrown in the garbage. It's too much. I can't let it happen. I have to get through to him *now*.

With no idea what else to try, I shove my face in so close to his that our noses almost touch. I virtually bore holes in his eyes with my stare, and concentrate so hard on finding a way to bring my voice out of the 'nothing' and into real life that I begin to feel dizzy.

"Shadow!"

It doesn't work. He doesn't stir. Not even a blink of recognition this time. Keep trying, I spur myself on. If you don't succeed, she will!

The horrible thoughts return. Shadow's lying on the steel table again. He's taking his last breaths. The room around him is dark, except for one beam of light shining in through a barred window and arrowing down on to his body. There's no one else around, just Shadow and I stuck together in some morbid dream. I can hear him wheezing, fighting for life. Specks of dust escape his coat and drift through the air. I can smell the pungent odour of all the other dogs who have lain here before him. It's so strong, so real, so overwhelming that it practically forces the words out of me. "SHADOW! WAKE UP!"

The volume of my voice seems to have a strength of its own. It echoes through the imaginary room, and where each echo hits the wall, a tiny crack appears. Slivers of light escape through the cracks. They shine in, not straight like they should be, but rolling like waves, carrying the sound away from the walls and down into Shadow's ears.

He flinches as each sound wave hits him, but when the echoes begin to peter out, the waves begin to roll slower, and Shadow doesn't wake up, I know I need to try harder.

I summon every inch of energy I can find. I conjure up every beautiful memory of our lives together and imagine all the things our future could hold. I clench my fists until they hurt, take a breath so deep it sucks in not only all the specks of dust in the room, but also the light shining around them, and at the top of my lungs, I scream as if it's the last thing I'll ever do.

"SHADOW! YOU NEED TO WAKE UP NOW."

My voice comes out like a sledgehammer. It slams into the walls and obliterates them like the flimsy figments of my imagination that they are. Light floods the room. The steel table vanishes beneath Shadow's body and is replaced by the wooden floorboards of Claire's veranda. Shadow's head flies up, as though shocked by the sudden brightness, and for the first time since my accident, he allows the tip of his tail to flutter into a brief, uncertain wag.

He heard me.

Shadow's alert. His ears are pricked as high as they'll go and he's searching the emptiness around him. I can just about hear him asking, 'Where are you?'

Not wanting to waste another second, knowing every one of them is one closer to Claire's undoubted return, I stretch my hand out until it rests just above the tips of carpet-thick hair between his ears.

The desperation that pushed my voice out and crumbled the walls in my vision is still there. I can feel it consuming me like a tingling rush flowing from somewhere deep inside and prickling all the way down my arm. I slowly lower it and the sensation strengthens until my entire palm is now also alive with pins and needles.

I lower it further, through the tingling that becomes so intense it burns. It feels like a boundary designed to keep me here in the 'nothing' and separated from the world around me. I understand its purpose, respect it even, but right now I don't have time to obey it.

A car starts up next door.

"Focus, Lucy."

It rolls toward the road and turns in our direction.

"Ignore it."

I keep my hand steady, fighting the burn and the tingling that together make me want to scream. I grit my teeth, close my eyes and...wait...I think I feel something.

One tiny sensation, different from the tingling, lightly brushing against my quivering fingertips. I spread my fingers apart and stretch them down further. It's soft, it's recognisable...it's Shadow's hair.

In the split second it takes me to recognise what my fingertips can feel, the burning disappears. The tingling shoots back up my arm, encases my whole body and explodes outward, taking with it the boundary that separated me from the world.

I can feel the floorboards beneath my feet. I can feel the heat of the afternoon sun, and when I dare to open my eyes to look at my hand, I can see beneath it, only inches from my face and lightened by a million tiny flecks of hazelnut and certainty, Shadow's deep brown eyes. They're no longer looking through me – but directly at me.

"Shadow?" I whisper, caring less for the fact that his excited panting smells of rotten bone and more for the fact that I can actually smell it. "Shadow, can you really see me?"

Shadow's tail erupts into a full-blown assault on the floorboards. Yes, yes, yes, it says with each thump. He can't get to his feet fast enough and barges headfirst into my chest, gloriously almost knocking me over rather than falling straight through me. He practically bends himself in half, wriggling and writhing to fill every nook and cranny of my arms which, for the first time in a long time, I can finally throw around him again.

The 'nothing' is broken.

7

Run!

Shadow and I are once again together, and by the sound of tires rolling over gravel toward the house, not a minute too soon.

"Shadow, sshhh!" I warn, unfolding my arms from around him and propelling to my feet.

Acutely aware of the sudden shift in my behaviour, Shadow holds still, watching me with a readiness to act on my slightest notion.

The tires roll closer.

"Shadow, we've got to get out of here."

Expecting an irate Claire to storm the veranda at any moment, Shadow and I pick up our heels, hoping to make it out into the open before she has a chance to corner him. We reach the front of the house and dash down the steps with a flourish of premature confidence, one that shrivels into a horrified knot in the pit of my stomach as I swivel my eyes up to see something far worse than Claire.

Just ahead, where the yard's fence narrows onto the drive-way, leaving no room either side for an escape, stand reclusive next-door neighbours, father and son wannabe-pro-kangaroo-shooters Greg and Sam, looking like they've battered their way straight out of a backyard slaughterhouse.

I recognise the men only due to an encounter Mum and Claire had with a huge carpet snake a few weeks ago. I hated the idea of them then, for pointlessly killing such a magnificent and peacefully harmless creature, and I hate the idea of them now, for whatever it is they have in store for Shadow.

Neither look as though they've bothered to change clothes since the last time I saw them, both still barely covering their proud and hairy beer bellies with the same torn and conspicuously stained navy-blue singlets, both bulging over the sides of frayed football shorts that ride up as they walk, offering an icky peek a little too high up for anyone's good taste, and both slapping their dusty feet about in water-ski-sized thongs.

On their own, they ooze enough cruelty to earn a place in the dictionary under the title 'scum of the earth', but together with the heavily rust-flaked, roadkill-spattered, faded bottle-green ute blocking the driveway behind them, they utterly terrify me.

Shadow's taken the most inopportune time to feel nostalgic. Rather than stay close while I figure out a way around the two men, he's realised he's left his one keepsake behind – my jogger. Before I can stop him, he bounds back along the veranda to retrieve it.

"There he is, Sam." The father points straight through me, locking his sights on Shadow. "Look out though, ay. Claire reckons he's turned feral, bloody rotten bugger. She said he pretty much took her hand off. Grab that choker chain. We'll cut him off up the top there."

"Leave him alone!" I yell. But, unlike Shadow, the two men don't hear me. I bend down to pick up a handful of stones, it's the only weapon I can think of. My hand passes straight through them and comes back empty. How could I feel the floorboards before, and the sun, but not the stones now? I look down at my feet. The gravel beneath them should be sharp enough to hurt. It feels smooth and flat, like the wood on the veranda; the wood beneath *Shadow's feet*. Does that mean I can only feel what Shadow feels? What good am I if he is the only thing I can touch?

The scrape of metal on metal catches my attention. I lift my head to see the younger of the two men tugging at a length of chain lying in a messy heap on the ute's tray. Nothing about the chain, from its heavy-duty links to the oversized D-shackle welded onto one end, looks even remotely pet-store approved.

"Whataya wanna do with him," he asks his dad, "If we catch him, that is. He looks pretty quick."

"Told Claire we'd take him to the pound, but pretty sure we can save ourselves a drive, ay? Make good crab-pot bait, that one. Not much else you can do with a dog like that. If he's turned on her once, he'll do it again. Got the taste of blood now. Can't be saved."

The gravity of Greg's words hit me with a whack. I can't even think about Shadow being caught by these two monsters. I can't let it happen. We need to get out of here now more than ever.

On the top step, with jogger in mouth and no way past Greg and Sam's fast approaching blockade at the bottom, Shadow's guard is up. The growling Claire received is nothing compared to the noises he's making now. He understands the threat and is determined to get back by my side as quickly as possible, and to look as dangerous as possible doing it. With hackles on end from the top of his neck to the tip of his tail, Shadow's eyes dart from where I stand out in the yard to the two men, and back again. There's no way for him to get to me other than past the father and son.

Greg's leaning forward with his arms spread wide, ready to pounce and catch, while Sam's holding his home-made choker chain like a lasso.

Shadow's eyes flit toward me again, asking, begging me to tell him what to do. Frantically I search for another way round. If he were smaller, he could slip through the upright railing slats and jump to the ground. If he were bigger, he could climb over them. "You have to make a run for it, Shadow. Don't hesitate, just run!"

Greg braces himself. "He looks like he's gunna try and get past us. You got that chain ready?"

Sam widens the noose and holds it spread open, ready to slip over Shadow's neck. "Yep, good to go."

From somewhere off to my right, I hear the crow of Claire's voice. "Did you get him yet, Greg?"

It must have been *her* car I heard turning into next door, because she's now standing on Greg's side of the fence trying desperately to see up over it and toward her veranda. Her interruption creates a distraction for Greg and Sam and an opportunity for Shadow.

"Now, Shadow. RUN!"

All the power in Shadow's hind legs thrusts him into a dramatic lurch forward. Jogger still clutched between teeth, he doesn't take his eyes off his target – me.

With one massive bound, he's whipping between two sets of hairy male legs. Greg's reaction is quicker than expected. His right arm slams down hard and wraps around Shadow's chest. His left arm closes in behind, and for a terrifying moment, I think Shadow's about to be caught.

"The chain, Sam. Get it on him. NOW!"

Sam fumbles with the chain. He's not as quick or as confident as his dad, and Shadow's not making things any easier for him, thrashing, snarling, and frantically almost turning himself inside out to escape.

Greg's grip begins to come unstuck.

Sam tries desperately to slip the chain over Shadow's head before it's too late. "Hold him still, Dad. I can't get it while he's moving around like that."

He thinks he's got it and quickly drops the noose. He gives a mighty tug on the chain, throws himself off-balance and falls backward, dragging the choker chain with him, the noose end wrapped perfectly around his dad's wrist.

The force of Sam's falling weight rips Greg's arm away from Shadow and flings it backward with such thrust that I think I hear his shoulder pop. The chain around his wrist pulls tight enough to cut into his skin. Sam yanks on it one more time, thinking Shadow's neck is at the other end, but instead, it cuts deeper into Greg's wrist. Deep enough to say hello to all the tiny bones beneath.

Greg's bellowing is battlefield loud and he can't drop Shadow quick enough to wrap his other hand around the wound.

While Sam turns white after one glimpse at his dad's wrist, Shadow falls to the ground, lands on his feet, drops my jogger, and runs.

We don't turn around to see Greg's blood-covered wrist or the bruising. We don't pay any attention to Claire angrily shouting from behind the fence, "What's happening? Why did you let him go?"

Shadow and I are gone.

We are over the ute, down the driveway, out the wide-open gate and onto the road before Greg can even think to remove the choker chain from his wrist. Long before the son can usher his dad to their car and head for the hospital, Shadow and I are on our way to where he should have gone in the first place. We are on our way to Astrid.

***

We wait with pounding hearts, hiding in the shade of a gum tree far enough from the road to be out of sight, should anyone be searching. Shadow blinks up at me, glowing with the most contagious pride and contentment.

I know why I am here now. I may not be able to do any of the physical things I used to, but I can still lead.

I know now that I am here to protect Shadow and destined to stay until he is safe in his new home, the only home that was ever going to be right for him – Astrid's.

I know now that I am Shadow's angel.

8

Discoveries

We stay hidden until the roar of Greg's ute fades into the distance. Claire followed close behind, and with Babinda having its own emergency ward less than ten minutes away, I figure now is the time to make our move.

The road we are on is the only way out. Both sides gutter onto endless paddocks filled with fat cows and even fatter horses that lift their heads and halt mid-chew to watch Shadow pass by. On a normal walk, Shadow would be trotting ahead and chasing scents all over the place. Today he remains by my side in the middle of the deserted street. He times his pace to keep with mine, and in the afternoon stillness I can hear the clicking of his rounded claws as they scratch the tops of the tiny stones embedded into the bitumen. Every so often, he looks up at me as if to check I'm still here. Each time he does, I reach down and touch his head, just to check I can still feel him.

I remember from previous Claire visits that we should eventually intersect with a service road which runs parallel to the highway and heads south. South's where we want to get to – a long, long, long way south – Echuca, Victoria south. Since I have no other ideas on how to get there, that road is as good a place to start as any.

***

It's dusk by the time we reach the turn-off, and I'm a nervous wreck. Spending hours on such an open road, with barely any places for Shadow to hide, had me panicking over everything that sounded even remotely like a car. I kept expecting to see either Greg and Sam or Claire drive past. I kept imagining them pulling over, chasing and catching Shadow, but luck was on our side and there was no sign of them anywhere.

With the sky turning a deep rosewood pink and the risk vanishing of anyone we know spotting us, we turn into unfamiliar territory, slow our pace, and finally begin to relax.

There's not a breath of wind. The chorus of chirping crickets that fills the warm evening air reminds me of countless afternoons spent lying with Shadow on the grass in our old backyard. We'd watch the trees turn into shadowy silhouettes, see the first stars come out, bask in the warmth of the earth underneath us, and I'd wish summer would never end.

I can feel that same warmth on my skin now. I'm getting hungry too, not to mention so thirsty I could drink a whole jug of water in one gulp. I know I don't need food anymore, water either, but Shadow does. So just like the floorboards under my feet, I can gather that these feelings are obviously not my own.

***

It's been hours since the sun went down, and my new empty stomach and dry mouth have become an obsession. I never realised quite how much water Shadow drank before. I always just made sure there was plenty available. Now that there's none though, and I can *feel* it, it's really sinking in. The hunger isn't so bad yet. I know Shadow hasn't been fed since this morning, but neither Mum nor Claire were very generous feeders, so I'm wondering if it's nothing more than the norm.

As we walk in silence, following a quarter moon offering just enough light to distinguish the road from the surrounding paddocks, I wonder how much of what Shadow feels will extend to me. If he feels pain, will I feel it too? What if he eats another rotten bone – and I can taste it!

I already know there's hunger, thirst, the warmth of the sun this afternoon; there'll probably be cold too. I felt the floorboards he was standing on, but not Greg's arm earlier, nor my hand when I touch him. It must be a well-being thing. Maybe I can only feel the things that keep Shadow comfortable and alive.

He looks up at me for another just making sure you're still there check. As he does his mouth falls into an open smile and I catch a whiff of his breath. The odour makes me gag.

"Well-being or not, Shadow, how about we stay away from rotten bones: just in case, hey?"

The latest sensory discovery keeps me occupied as we plod further and further along our service road. Soon enough, the tiring events of such a traumatic and unanticipated day catch up to us. Shadow's feet begin to drag and his head hangs so low that his drooping tongue only barely avoids scraping the ground.

There's a soft patch of grass between two gum trees on our left. I lead him into the thickest part and as soon as he falls asleep, I notice how my mind and body starts to recharge. After everything I've learned, about how closely we are now connected, I think it's safe to say if Shadow dies, I die – again.

***

Before the first tinge of yellow seeps into an early morning sky, Shadow has shaken free of a build-up of overnight dew and we are on our way again. We walk with pace through the cool of dawn, skip between tree shadows to escape the sting of the midday sun, and trundle on into the afternoon humidity.

Over the course of the day, our service road deviates both toward and away from the highway. Sometimes so close we feel the whoosh from passing traffic, other times so far we can't even hear it and can only hope to still be heading in the right direction.

"Be good if you were a cow," I say, an effort to raise my spirits up and away from the grip of hunger that has considerably tightened since last night. "Everything's so green. You'd never starve."

The joke is lost on Shadow, and on me, if I'm honest. It succeeds only in making me realise the cluelessness with which I am leading both of us toward something we may never find.

We've only been walking for *one* day. Who knows how many more there'll be, and already the thought of, how *will* I find him food, is doing more than just playing on my mind, it's starting to bring me down. I can't buy it. I can't ask anyone. I can't make it. I can't even pick it up to steal it!

Yesterday's optimism begins to dwindle. Doubt creeps in, takes hold, and stops me in my tracks.

"What are we doing, Shadow? This is stupid. It's something like three thousand kilometres. Three THOUSAND! I've never been further than a few hours drive out of Cairns. How am I supposed to take you all the way to Victoria?"

Shadow halts beside me. Lightly panting, he tilts his head upward. His eyes are as clear and carefree as the day I met him. There's none of my worry to be found in them. No fear or concern, only an image of he and I together, as though out for a Sunday stroll.

"It's going to be a majorly long stroll, Shadow. Like the longest stroll ever."

He brushes off my negativity with a blink and resumes his puppy-dog stare. I want to look away. I've already plummeted down into a little hole of self-pity and I don't feel like climbing back out again just yet, but Shadow's eyes have a grip on me that I can't seem to break free from. In them, I still see the same picture – he and I together, out for a stroll. Only the longer I continue to stare, the more detailed the picture becomes.

It filters into my mind the same way a dream would. We're on a bitumen road, just as we are now, but we're not alone. Astrid is there. She's crying, but it doesn't feel sad. In fact, it feels strangely – euphoric: as though we've all been anxiously waiting for something that's finally about to arrive.

It's just an image, but the associated feeling is real enough to pull me out of the depths of my distress and leave me questioning. "Is that a vision, Shadow, or just a hope?"

Shadow relaxes his stare and the image fades. He grins impossibly wide, swipes his tail from side to side, then starts ahead. When I don't immediately follow, he stops, and I swear that if he had eyebrows, then I would say he raises them at me as if to say, well, we won't find out standing here now, will we?

9

Biscuits

It feels like forever since our service road met and then glued itself to a seemingly endless stretch of needle-straight highway. With no variations in sight (outside of a sign I saw a while back saying Tully 20 k), there's little to distract from the monotony. Placing one foot in front of the other has now become an increasingly boring chore.

Although the vast majority of the roadside is litter-free, every now and then we spot a crumpled paper bag from one fast food restaurant or another. Hoping for leftovers, Shadow investigates each bag thoroughly, and so far has been lucky enough to find a bite-sized portion of some kind of burger patty, and a couple of soggy chips. Thankfully, while I felt them fill the tiniest bit of the hole in my stomach, I tasted neither.

He darts off the road again now for a bright blue, hard plastic container with a press-on lid. It could have once been a biscuit jar, maybe one of those oversized novelty ones. The lid is still on and the larger bottom end has been chewed through in a couple of places by rats or mice. Shadow's fairly happy with his find, and when I look through the small chew holes, I can see there are indeed a couple of biscuits inside.

Listening only to his hunger, Shadow nudges the jar with his nose. Having no luck, he tries prodding, and then dragging it toward himself with his paw.

"You need to get the lid off," I tell him, but of course he doesn't understand and continues to fumble.

"The lid, Shadow." I point to it.

Shadow stops what he's doing to study the lid, making me wonder if I can show him, just the way he showed me his vision of Astrid earlier. He knows a lot of words that I've taught him over the years, but not enough for him to be able to understand me completely. If I can communicate with him through pictures though, I'd be able to tell *or show* him anything!

I point again to the lid. This time, instead of saying anything, I picture him tearing it off with his teeth.

He cranes his neck up at me as though I'm speaking. Then with more accuracy than I could have anticipated, he wraps his teeth around the rim of the lid, exactly as I pictured.

He saw my thoughts!

Shadow got the biscuits. I was so drawn into the possibilities of our newfound form of communication that I forgot to watch him as closely as I should have. While I was busy thinking about all the things I could show him, he yanked the lid off, pushed the jar around with his nose until it tipped forward and stood upright. He then squeezed his head down through the tight rim, all the way up to his neck.

That was about an hour ago and his head is still inside the jar. It's completely stuck!

I have no idea what to do. I tried showing him with my thoughts how to grip the jar with his legs and pull it off, but it wouldn't budge. I tried searching for something to wedge the jar between, so all he would have to do is pull backwards, but there were two major problems: one, I couldn't find anything suitable, and two, Shadow can't see where he's going.

So here we sit, me racking my brain for a solution, and Shadow with his head stuck in a bright blue plastic jar.

"We'll just have to keep moving," I say.

The jar turns in my direction.

"I guess it could have been worse. There might not have been any holes in the bottom of it, and then you wouldn't be able to breathe."

The jar flops back to the ground and I hear a heavy sigh from within.

"I'll just keep talking and you can follow my voice. I saw it once on a game show and it worked really well."

Shadow, the bright blue plastic jar, and I make slow progress. I talk as constantly as I can, imagining and wondering out loud about everything from what Astrid's house might look like and whether or not Claire is out searching for Shadow, to the state of Greg's arm, and if Mum knows that Shadow is missing. When there's nothing left to speculate on, I try singing.

Staying in tune was never one of my strong points and each new song I start somehow ends up sounding exactly the same as the last, only with different words. I wouldn't have thought it would be an issue, but as I'm about to launch into my fifth song, I hear a very obvious 'oh please, not another one' groan escape through the holes in Shadow's jar.

"Oh, come on," I appeal. "I'm not *that* bad."

Shadow clearly disagrees. He throws himself to the ground and brings both front paws up to cover either side of the jar.

"Oh, you little bugger! Are you seriously trying to block your ears?"

He barks a muffled, but extremely cheeky yes.

"Wow! Exaggerate much? Bit rough, don't you think?"

I wait for some sign of guilt. A tail-wag, a bark, an I'm sorry whimper; but no, Shadow does the opposite and closes his paws tighter around the jar.

"*Ok* then," I have no choice but to give in, "I'll stop. Just come on, get up. We need to keep moving."

From there on, I fill the silence by explaining everything I see in full detail. It's not an easy task, given the unchanging landscape, and before long my explanations have whittled down to nothing more than flat-toned, one-word descriptions: "Tree. Car. Bird. Truck. Motorbike."

Eventually that too becomes an effort, and by the time our road finally deviates away from the highway toward the first signs of the upcoming 'Tully' suburbia, the most I can manage is a toneless grunt to accompany each laboured step.

10

It's a boy!

Almost twenty-four hours after leaving Claire's, Shadow and I turn off our service road toward the tiny town of Tully. Exhausted and aching all over, we ease our way onto a welcoming street of wooden-stumped houses that, although all neat and tidy with weatherboard walls painted in a variety of tropical-climate shades, could possibly pre-date the dawn of time.

As we make our way along the street I hear the laughter of children playing somewhere in a backyard, and from the front porch of the house immediately to our left, the unmistakable aroma of fresh-out-of-the-oven baked goods wafts toward us.

Lifting my nose to the deliciously sweet smell, I trace it back to a plate of muffins sitting on a small round table between a man and woman of around my grandparents' age. The man, dressed more like he's ready to go to a rodeo rather than waiting for the plate of muffins to cool down, is smirking at the woman, who although extremely fit looking for her mid-sixties age, still seems to have lost some sort of battle with the flour in the kitchen.

She's patting down her white-dusted, supposed-to-be black gym clothes, while the man's reaching in for a muffin despite their warning of rising steam. The woman cautions him against it, but with one eyebrow raised and half a smile, it comes across more like a dare. "You'll burn your mouth, George."

He seems determined to prove her wrong, even though he has to handball the muffin back and forth to stop it from burning his fingers. "Holy hell, that's hot," he pipes, before peeling his lips out of danger and defiantly biting off a chunk. His regret is instant and he resembles an ape as he throws the remainder back to the plate to fan his mouth. "Ah, ooh, ooh, ooh!"

"Told you," is the only pity he receives before the woman's attention is drawn to where Shadow and I watch from the street. She points our way and squints. "George, what's that?"

"What's what?" he muffles around his steaming mouthful.

"That there, on the street. It looks like ... it looks like that biscuit jar we lent the Kelly's' kids a while ago."

The man stops fanning. Intrigued, he stands up as if it'll help him see better. "Well, I'll be buggered."

"What, George? Where's my glasses?"

George's "Same place they always are, dear," seems like it's been said even more times than the woman's "Oh! I knew that," as she gropes at a pair of glasses hanging around her neck.

When she's done scoffing at herself, she asks George,

as though he should somehow know the answer, "George, what's our biscuit jar doing on that dog's head?"

George's chuckle is baritone deep. "Well, I can honestly say," he confesses. "I never thought I'd see that! How do you suppose he can see where he's going?"

"Don't laugh at the poor thing, George."

The woman's comment only makes George chuckle harder. "Come on now, Rosie, you have to admit you never expected your biscuit jar to be returned like that, did you?"

Rosie sees the funny side. "No, I guess not. We should probably get it off him. Whose dog do you think it is?"

George scans the street for an owner. "Haven't seen him before, but then most dogs here don't usually get around with jars on their heads either. Maybe the Kellys got a dog for the kids."

"No, I was only talking to Ruth yesterday. It's not theirs." Rosie gives herself a minute before concluding, "Nope, it's definitely not anyone's here."

George's smirk is back. "And you should know."

"What's that supposed to mean?"

"Nothing, dear," he answers sweetly, before starting toward Shadow on heavily bowed legs. "Nothing at all, nosy Rosie."

"George!"

Their banter carries them all the way down a white pebble path and out onto the street.

"How do you plan to get it off him, George?"

"I'll hold one end, you take the other, and then we'll both pull."

"What if he bites you after you pull the jar off?"

"All under control, dear; I'll pull the end that doesn't bite."

"George!"

Not wanting to scare Shadow, George quietly talks to him as he nears.

Shadow takes a step back. "It's okay," I tell him. "They're trying to help you."

He stays still while George pulls the legs of his jeans up enough to squat unhindered. The worn leather of his cowboy boots creases around his ankles as he reaches one calloused hand toward the holes in the bottom of the jar. "I'm not going to hurt you," he continues to soothe.

Shadow sniffs as best he can through the holes and finally gives a tail wag of approval.

Rosie feels the need to look presentable for their guest and runs through a quick fluff-up of her silver pixie-cut before bending down to follow George's lead.

Shadow shows his approval a second time, allowing the couple to begin discussing how to go about freeing him.

"See, dear?" George seems happy to be proven right. "I told you he wouldn't bite. Now grab hold of that jar and I'll pull his back legs."

"You can't just pull on his legs, George; you might stretch him."

George's look says more than enough.

"Oh, you know what I mean. He might put something out, just like you did when you tried doing those three Jazzercise videos in a row that time. Remember that, George? It was right after we left the farm and you were so lost for something to do, you took up aerobics." Now Rosie is chuckling.

George grumbles under his breath, and with a wave of

his hand, dismisses his wife's comment. "You're just jealous because of that whole blue spandex pants thing. *You* made me wear them, remember? You wanted us to go jogging together and thought we should wear matching outfits, like that crazy couple you're always watching on TV. But then you got cranky because I looked better in them than you did."

Rosie nearly chokes on her own laughter. "Mrs. Golding down the road didn't think so! Especially when you bent over to touch your toes right in front of her while she was bringing her wheelie bin in. Poor woman! Will probably never get over having to witness *that* from behind."

George grumbles again and wraps his arms around Shadow's chest. "Just pull the jar, for goodness' sake, would you?"

"Ah, no come back, hey? Alright, alright." Rosie places her hands either side of the jar. "Ready, George?"

"Ready."

She pulls on the jar, gently at first, and then realising it's not going to budge so easily, she gives it a little more effort. "Pull him back toward you, George. I can't do everything myself, you know."

George puts his back into it and pulls Shadow like a calf being born the wrong way round. Rosie pulls harder as well and Shadow thrashes his head, almost ripping the jar from Rosie's grasp.

"Don't let it go, woman; it's nearly off."

Rosie gives one final yank and with a dull, popping sound, Shadow bursts out of the jar and into the daylight.

"It's a boy!" George trumpets, stumbling backward and taking Shadow with him.

A minute of disorientated rapid blinking later, Shadow sees his helpers for the first time. Unable to decide who to thank first, he darts between George and Rosie, gratefully licking, yelping, and all but wiping them out with the whip of his tail.

Righting himself, George decides, "He's probably thirsty. Who knows how long he's had that thing on his head?"

He leaves Rosie to inspect the jar, calling Shadow to follow as he starts toward the house. "Come on, boy. Let's get you taken care of, hey?"

11

'Maybe' isn't good enough

Shadow flakes out on his side the minute he makes it up onto the porch.

Rosie takes a pillow from her chair and uses it to soften the floor for herself next to him. "You're a beautiful boy, aren't you?" she says, shifting her bony backside into a comfortable position. "Where's your owner then, huh?"

Shadow's answer is a heavy pant and an eye shift in my direction. She's right here, he means to say. Can't you see her?

George heads into the house and soon returns with two bowls, one full of some kind of mince, the other with water. He thoughtfully places them close enough to Shadow's nose that they require only a roll onto his belly to reach, and in a matter of minutes, Shadow has the mince bowl licked clean and is all but choking from trying to drink too quickly.

"Bit hungry, hey, boy?" George comments. "What do you think, Rosie? Should we keep him here tonight? It's a bit late to go door-knocking now. We'll see if we can find his owner tomorrow?"

"Way too late for door-knocking." Rosie wholeheartedly agrees. "I've still got an old dog bed from the farm in the spare room. I'll pull it out in a minute."

Tiredness and a full belly drag Shadow back onto his side where his eyes almost instantly begin their struggle to stay open.

"Poor thing's knackered." Rosie strokes her hand along Shadow's body.

Her touch wrenches him out of his near comatose state long enough for their eyes to meet.

Rosie's face creases just like George's boots, taking on a frown of sympathy she seems sadly familiar with. "Two little lost souls," she murmurs.

George overhears. "What do you mean: two?"

"Oh, I was just thinking about Michael."

"Michael from down the road, or our Michael?"

"Why on earth would I be thinking about Michael from down the road?"

"Who knows with you."

Rosie's head rolls back as she tries to find her patience in the ceiling. "Our Michael, of course." Sympathy seeps back in. "Just something about this dog reminds me of him. Like...his innocence is gone. Do you think, George...Michael might...He's been through such a lot——"

George obviously knows exactly what Rosie is about to say. "Don't get ahead of yourself, dear." He cuts her off. "I'm sure someone will be missing that dog. We can't just go giving him away to someone else."

"Oh, he rang before." Rosie remembers. "Said he'd drop in tomorrow if he can. We should at least let them meet. Just in case we don't find an owner. Poor Michael: such a tough year. I bet he'd love a bit of company."

"Once again," George reiterates, "let's not get ahead of ourselves."

Rosie falls into silence for a moment, before saying, "Sometimes things are meant to be, you know, George. Maybe this little one picked our house for a reason. Stranger things have happened."

"He picked our house because he had a biscuit jar stuck on his head and couldn't see where he was going."

"Then maybe the *jar* picked our house."

George raises a mocking eyebrow at Rosie. "Yes, my dear, stranger things indeed."

***

Shortly after nightfall, the mosquitos chase Rosie and George off the porch and into the house.

George settles in to watch the news while Shadow and I follow Rosie to retrieve a large cushion with an embroidered paw in one corner from their spare room.

"This was our old Luna's bed," she tells Shadow. "She was more Michael's dog actually. Come to think of it, you look a bit like her. She made it to the ripe old age of sixteen before she went over the rainbow bridge. I'd love to get another dog."

I hear George from the lounge room. "Who are you talking to?"

"Who do you think?" Rosie calls back.

She leads us into where George lazes reclined in front of the tv. She fluffs up the dog bed on the floor with the same enthusiasm as her hair earlier, then sinks into her own recliner before purposely raising her voice over that of the news reader. "I know *George* would love a dog too. He won't admit it though. He makes excuses about it being too difficult when we go caravanning."

"That's because it will be!" George ups the tv volume, attempting to end the conversation.

His attempt fails as Rosie raises her voice to match. "I know *heaps* of grey nomads with dogs. Besides, chances are we'll never even get a caravan."

"Money doesn't grow on trees," George retorts.

Rosie slumps in resignation. Shadow follows her lead and stretches out on the dog bed. The news reader babbles on with no further disturbances, and as Shadow begins to fall asleep, Rosie smiles down at him with the same sympathy she did on the porch. "Those eyes," she says. "I wonder what you've been through. I hope you'll get to meet Michael tomorrow."

She turns her attention to the tv, so I lay down beside Shadow and rest my arm across his belly. Michael must be their son, I assume, conjuring up an image of a man who, judging by Rosie and George's age, must be somewhere around forty. "Would you like to stay here tomorrow and meet him? Maybe Rosie's right. Maybe the 'biscuit' jar did lead us here."

Shadow opens his eyes and rolls them mockingly at me, as

if he's been taking lessons from George. He sweeps aside my indistinct image of Michael and returns one of Astrid.

"Understood," I say. "I guess maybe isn't good enough."

***

Rested and reenergised, Shadow and I slip out of Rosie and George's street before dawn. With a little guidance, the brass handle of their unlocked front door was a breeze for Shadow to pull down. Before leaving, I'd spotted a tiny porcelain figurine on the coffee table in the living room. The figurine was of a young girl in a blue dress and wide-brimmed straw hat holding a droopy-eared puppy in her arms. Wanting somehow to show our appreciation to the couple for their kindness, I showed the figurine to Shadow and asked him if he could pick it up without breaking it.

As careful as could be, he pinched it between his teeth and carried it to the bed he'd spent the night on.

I don't know if the couple will understand the gesture, but it was the most Shadow and I were capable of.

12

The rescue

With Tully now behind us and our service road laid out in front, we fall back into the same picture as yesterday morning: wide open paddocks on either side, grazing cattle and horses all around, a blinding sun to our left.

By the afternoon, the increasing panting and drooping of Shadow's tongue, along with a damp, sticky feeling over my skin, tells me the humidity is building, and one look to the west tells me why.

Like an army rolling in from some distant land, a thick front of charcoal grey clouds is forming. It's still a distance away, but I can already feel it sucking in the wind around us to strengthen its forces.

Shadow hates storms. By now he'd usually be preparing to bunker down under my bed, but there won't be any bed tonight.

"I hate to say it, Shadow, but we might just have to tough this one out."

***

Dotted here and there between the gums and flat, grassy

paddocks, sunburnt tin roofs send heat waves shimmering into the sky. The closest sits at the end of a long dirt driveway.

It doesn't appear to be any different from the other roofs, but something about it causes Shadow to lift his nose in the direction of the wooden house beneath.

"What can you smell?" I ask.

Following his nose, Shadow veers off the road and starts down the driveway.

It doesn't feel safe. "Shadow!" I call out. "Shadow, wait!"

Shadow stops abruptly and turns to face me. He wags his tail with a confidence that says trust me, lets out a series of beckoning barks and carries on without waiting any longer.

While I don't understand why he is heading toward the house when I am certain he senses the same danger I feel, he doesn't bother to stop again leaving me no choice but to race to catch up.

Shadow's pace picks up, and before long we are staring up at a house so dilapidated, it's hard to imagine it ever had a heyday. Patches of paint have peeled off the outer walls, the stumps have been chewed through by termites, the windows are smashed, and the front door is hanging by only one hinge and swinging wide open

The overgrown lawn is no better off. It's not only so long that I can barely find Shadow in it, it's also littered with old car parts and household rubbish. All together, it looks like the kind of place squatters might use from time to time.

"Why did you want to come here?" I ask Shadow.

The first whispers of the oncoming storm sweep their way around the side of the house, sending the tips of the grass around us bending backwards in the breeze. As they do, I hear something that doesn't belong on this obviously deserted property, a sound so sad and lonely it can't be ignored. I hear a whimper. I now understand what drew Shadow here, but I still feel the need to ask, "How on earth did you hear that from out there on the street?"

One of Shadow's ears flicks backward toward a suspicious rustle in the grass.

"That answers that," I joke. "Surround sound with those things, huh?"

I hear the rustle again, a little closer. "Come on, Shadow, let's get out of here. If that's a snake and you get bitten, we're done."

Slightly more nervous than I'd like to be, I follow Shadow as he blindly fights his way through the grass toward the whimper. I don't know if it's Shadow's feelings, my own, or those of the poor creature that lies ahead, but as we get closer to the sound, I notice a loneliness begin to take over me.

It grows stronger and stronger, engulfing my heart and weighing me down. It's worse than any loneliness I can ever remember feeling. It's as if there's nothing outside of it, as if I can't imagine it ever ending because I don't know anything different. By the time we break through the last blades, it has consumed me. I can no longer remember what happiness is. My whole world just feels like one giant pit of despair.

When I then see the source of the whimper, I understand why.

Tethered by a chain wrapped a dozen times around the crooked pole of an overhead clothesline, gazing through milky-white eyes and looking utterly defeated by the world, lies an old, forgotten dog. The patch of ground beneath the cracked and bleeding pads of his paws is trodden to dust, and his coat of bristly orange is faded from an unfathomable amount of unrelenting sun, wind, and rain.

Shadow cautiously approaches, motivating the dog to pull itself through a painful groan to its feet.

I notice 'it' is a 'he' and almost have to turn my eyes away from the sight of so many sharp bones protruding through hanging skin. His condition is so poor it takes me a while to figure out his Labrador breed.

As Shadow nears, the old dog takes a shaky step forward, whereby the chain instantly tightens around his neck. He seems to know better than to fight against it and submissively drops back to the ground.

Shadow meets my eyes with a whimper of his own. Help him, I know he is pleading.

"I don't know if I can," I say. "No one except you can see me, remember?"

Just try, Shadow's next whimper begs.

"I will," I promise, preparing myself for the whole tingling and burning process again.

I step closer to the old dog, and just as it did a moment ago, loneliness fills my heart.

If I can feel *that*, I think, maybe fighting my way through the boundary *once* was enough. I didn't feel anything from Rosie and George, but humans are probably a bit closed off to – things like me. Maybe when I connected with Shadow, I opened myself up to be seen by other animals as well. After all, they don't have society telling them what's real and not real.

The thought sounds plausible. It's worth testing. So, as calmly as if I were talking to Shadow, I ask the Lab, "Can you hear me?"

The Lab lifts his head, as though unsure if his floppy, mange-covered ears are playing a trick on him.

The despair in my heart subsides just a little. "Can you hear me, old boy?" I ask again.

This time his milky eyes turn toward me and his tail makes a slow, but acknowledging trail through the dust.

How about that, I think. Once *was* enough!

Not entirely sure of what to do next, but knowing I can communicate with Shadow through images, I try picturing the Lab standing up. He groans louder than the first time and shudders through the effort, but he follows my thoughts and stands.

"You need to loosen the chain to get free," I say, wishing I were able to do it for him.

I reach down and place my hand on his head. There's no tingling or burning, just wiry tufts of hair, patchy skin, and a rounded skull beneath. I picture the chain around his neck, a simple choker chain that tightens when pulled on. I imagine the Lab stepping back toward the pole and the chain loosening.

He sees what I am asking him to do and begins to move backwards, but clogged with rust, the chain doesn't loosen nearly as much as I'd hoped.

"Shadow," I call, "we need your help."

I remember Shadow's favourite game of tug-o-war and tell him to pull on the chain around the Lab's neck. With the usual excitement in his step, Shadow bounds into the game.

"Gentle," I warn, and Shadow listens.

The chain between Shadow's teeth pulls away from the old dog's neck, revealing patches of skin that are rubbed bare in some places, and broken and bleeding in others.

Fighting the urge to ask what is *wrong* with some people, I instead picture the Lab stepping further back and Shadow pulling further forward. Both coordinate their efforts perfectly and a second later, the Lab wriggles his way to freedom.

Clearly proud of himself, Shadow drops the chain and spins toward me for his well-done pat. The Lab, although no longer restricted, still seems stuck, and my heart fills again with loneliness. "You've got nowhere to go, have you?"

I don't need to do any sort of search of the area to know there's nothing and no one here that can help. I'd more than happily take him with us, but there's no way he'd make the trip. He needs food, water, a soft bed, a vet, love. He needs – oh my god, of course! He needs Rosie and George!

***

Coaxing the Lab away from his circle of dust, I cringe at how tentatively he places one cracked paw in front of the other. "Please let him have the strength," I pray, calling him further until he begins to follow on his own.

His legs warm out of their stiffness by the time we reach the road, and although in obvious pain, he soldiers on alongside Shadow and I as if he knows exactly what awaits if he can make the trip.

By nightfall, the menacing army of charcoal clouds has rolled in close enough to begin blocking out the stars. The moon eventually disappears and soon after, the first bolt of lightning flashes across the sky. When the thunder starts to rumble, Shadow tucks his tail in tight and attempts to push his way in to hide between my feet.

The old dog on my left trundles on unfazed. I hate to think of how many furious summer storms he must have weathered alone, chained to a clothesline on a sorry patch of dirt with no shelter and nothing but a pole to hide behind. I hate to think of his life prior to today or the reasons he would have for feeling safer tonight, with us, than maybe ever before.

***

The storm threatens us for hours. As soon as it seems the lightning might be subsiding and we might finally be able to carry on in peace, the rain sets in. Only isolated drops fall at first, one over here and a second or two later, another over there. They're huge drops, as big as my toe. Big ole fat rain, as Dad used to say.

It's as still as anything for a few minutes. Just long enough for Shadow to think it's safe to untangle himself from my legs. Then the wind starts up.

With a gust that could blow a tent over, it smashes into us and whips its way through the surrounding trees. A barrage of hard, driving rain comes along for the ride, instantly soaking the coats of my two companions and forcing them to turn their heads to one side to be able to see.

Shadow wants to stop. He's well and truly had enough of this storm now. I can tell, because as he looks up at me through half-squinted eyes, a picture of him hiding under my old bed pops straight into my mind.

"I'm sorry!" I have to shout through the wind and rain for him to hear me. "I wish I could take you back there, but I can't."

Feeling overwhelmed with pity, I slide down into the mud now guttering our bitumen road and drag Shadow's saturated body into my arms. The old dog approaches from the side and sticks his nose toward my face. He sniffs inquisitively, checking out my eyes, mouth and hair, his cold, wet nose gently poking and prodding me as it moves around.

"When was the last time anyone hugged you, old boy?" I hate but feel the need to ask.

The only answer I get is a head tilt of confusion.

"Oh, come here then, you poor thing."

Shadow thankfully shows no signs of jealousy as I unwrap an arm from him and use it to draw the old Lab in closer. Both dogs squeeze close to my sides as though I might offer some kind of protection, and as we huddle together I can't help but imagine the sight we must make. Three drowned rats, in the middle of the night, in the pouring rain, miles and miles from anywhere: just Shadow, an old abandoned dog, and a ghost.

It's a laughable picture. A pitifully cold, wet, and miserable one, but laughable all the same. And together with the wind howling, the mud sticking, and the road laid out like a clean-washed blank slate before us, the whole situation is also strangely – exhilarating.

Without fear of being heard, or a thought for anything else beyond this moment, I throw my head back to shout into the pitch-black sky above, "We're together, Shadow! Who cares where we are. We're together!"

13

Back again

At dawn, my eyes lock on to a familiar white pebble path leading up to a porch with cane chairs and a small round table.

Shadow trots confidently ahead, climbs the front steps and is greeted by the same two bowls he so gratefully emptied during our last visit. I watch him lap thirstily at the replenished water, and on closer inspection, notice the second bowl sits once again filled to the brim with mince.

My eyes catch sight of a small figurine placed snugly between the two bowls. The young porcelain girl and her droopy-eared puppy smile back at me and it warms my heart to see that Rosie and George have understood our gesture of thanks.

Shadow quenches his thirst and sniffs the mince. He's hungry, I know, but he doesn't touch it. Instead, as I watch and glow with pride, he turns to the old dog and beckons him with a soft bark.

I can almost hear the Lab's bones rattle, so violent is his shaking. The brave face with which he soldiered on throughout the night has been replaced by one that winces in pain. His skin seems to hang deeper into the crevices between his bones than it did yesterday, and the worn pads of his cracked and bleeding paws threaten him to dare take another step.

I wish I could carry him over the finish line, but urging him on is the best I can do. "Go on, boy. You've come this far."

Gathering every last scrap of strength, he heaves his exhausted body up onto the porch, where Shadow sits by the two bowls thumping his tail noisily against the floor. Eat, he demands. Eat!

Within minutes, the water bowl is empty and the last sliver of mince is gobbled up. A light clicks on inside the house and the front door opens to a familiar figure hugged by *blue* gym clothes this time, but styled all the same like she's ready for guests at any hour. It is of course, Rosie.

"George! George, quick," Rosie yells through the house. "I was just about to go for my walk, but the dog's back and..." She stops at the sight of the old dog.

"And what?" I hear George from somewhere inside.

"Well, he's brought a friend, but – oh dear."

"Oh dear, what? Is it that fishing rod I lent Gary last week? It's not broken, is it?"

"*No*, George, just come and have a look."

George appears beside his wife in under-eye-bags and saggy-crotched pyjamas that together are a far cry from the cowboy we met last time. He yawns at Shadow like his return wasn't worth getting up for, but changes his tune the second he lays eyes on the old dog. "Crikey mate, you've seen better days!"

Rosie's straight to the verge of crying. "Oh, the poor thing looks like he hasn't eaten in weeks."

With a tenderness I don't expect George shows often, he rubs Rosie's shoulder and assures her, "It's alright, dear. I'll get him something."

He takes the two bowls and slips inside. When he returns both are full again, and Shadow waits patiently while the old dog fits a bit more into his stomach before taking to the remainder of the mince. George, in the meantime, disappears inside, presumably before the world has the chance to realise he's not a cowboy anymore.

Belted, booted and buttoned when he swaggers back out, the tenderness is gone and he's straight down to business. "So, now we have *two* owners to find. I'll leave that up to you, Rosie dear."

"I hardly think the skinny one has an owner, George, and if he does, then they've done a disgusting job of looking after him."

"Now, now, let's not jump to conclusions. Maybe he's just been missing for a long time. He's had a feed now. He could probably do with a good sleep and a flea bath too, I'd say. When the shops open, I'll run down and see what they've got in the way of shampoo for him."

"We should probably take him to the vet, don't you think?" Rosie suggests.

"It's too early. Besides, he doesn't look like he wants to do much more than sleep today anyway. No different to Luna when she got lost mustering that time. Why don't we let him do that. Provided the two of them don't go walkabout again before tomorrow, we'll take them both to the vet and see if they've got those chip things they stick in their necks these days."

Rosie runs her eyes over the old dog again and says, "I might ring the vets when they open anyway. Just in case. I'll describe his condition and see what they say."

"I'm pretty sure they'll tell you the same. But you do whatever you want, dear. You're going to anyway."

With the Lab now fully discussed, Rosie turns her attention back to Shadow. "Don't you think it's strange, George?"

"What?"

"Well, this one turning up two days ago. Somehow figuring out how to open our front door and sneaking out yesterday morning. Leaving that figurine on the bed! Now here he is again with another dog that needs help. It's almost like – like he knows what he's doing, like he brought this other dog especially to us."

"Did he know what he was doing when he got our jar stuck on his head?"

"I'm serious, George. I wouldn't be surprised if he's picked the old boy up somewhere along the way and thought I know just the place for you. Unless – now don't laugh, George, because this will sound crazy – but unless they're not *alone*."

The washed-out hazel of Rosie's eyes warms to a ginger-nut brown with the hope. They hunt through the air until they line up with mine, and for a second my heart skips a beat as I think she sees me. They don't hold their position though, and when they fix themselves on an empty space a little to my right, I know that all she sees is her own belief.

"Thank you," she says, speaking to something *she's* not even sure exists. "Whoever you are, you're an angel."

"I'm Shadow's angel," I say aloud, wanting desperately for her to hear me.

My heart skips about fifty beats when she bursts out, "Shadow! George, the name Shadow just popped into my head. I *told* you they're not alone. How else would I come up with such a specific name?"

She leans in close to Shadow. "Is that your name?" she asks, taking every blink as a sign of recognition.

I tell Shadow to speak, but he's too tired for games, leaving Rosie disappointed and without anything conclusive.

George, who sceptically watched for Shadow's reaction from the sidelines, huffs an "Of course not," under his breath, then fetches a familiar dog bed and an old blanket which he lays, side by side, on the floor.

Within minutes, both Shadow and the old dog are snoring rhythmically beside each other and another long night has finally come to an end.

***

I lull around on the porch with Rosie and George while I wait for Shadow to feel rested enough to continue.

Throughout the day, Rosie keeps herself entertained by fluttering around in her garden of desert roses, preparing meals and snacks, and stretching her Lycra into every precarious position her online yoga class has to offer. She phones

the vet and receives the same answer as George predicted –
sleep, food, a bath, and bring him in tomorrow.

George makes a quick trip to the store for flea shampoo,
then returns to spend a good hour washing, soaking, massag-
ing, rinsing, and hand-towelling the old dog. After his bath,
the old dog goes back to his blanket and George hides himself
behind a newspaper.

He reads it front to back, twice, both times intermittently
calling upon Rosie to either "Listen to this idiot," or, "Check
this out. What'll they think of next?" He picks out caravans
from the classifieds section and reads their descriptions to
Rosie, who replies each time with the same complaint: "Too
expensive, I'm afraid."

I listen as they speak through mouthfuls of sandwich
about their son, Michael, bicker about where to grey nomad
to first, and wonder aloud about the individual lives of
Shadow and the Lab leading up to this point.

Eventually another beautiful dusk sets in. It's the fourth
since we left Claire's, and dismally enough, we haven't even
made it one hundred kilometres from the house yet. When I
think of how far we've still got to go, I feel less than encour-
aged: three thousand kilometres. I'd rather not think about it,
or about how impossible it seems.

***

Shadow wakes first as the evening mosquitoes return. He
spends a good amount of time chasing their buzzing around
and trying to snatch them out of mid-air, but there's too
many for him to keep up with. Hoping I'll swat them away
for him, he scampers across the porch to where I sit in the

'empty' chair beside Rosie and anchors his pleading eyes on mine.

Rosie doesn't miss a beat. "I wish I could see you," she says, following Shadow's stare with certainty. "I know you're there; your presence surrounds your dog and I've been able to feel you here all day. I can't explain how, it's just a feeling, or a knowing rather, as though I'm not alone."

"You're not alone," George butts in. "I'm here, aren't I?"

"That's different, George. Obviously I know *you're* here, but I know someone else is here too."

She turns back to my chair, unsure of exactly where to look. "He's a lucky dog to have his very own angel."

"I hope I can live up to such a divine expectation," I reply, knowing the time has come for me to lead Shadow back out into the great unknown. "I really hope so."

Rosie reaches down to give Shadow a pat. "I guess there was a reason you came here after all," she says, glancing at the old dog. "I thought maybe you were supposed to meet Michael, but he didn't get a chance to stop in, and even if he had, you weren't here anyway."

Shadow sees me stand and removes himself from Rosie's touch. He takes himself over to the old dog, briefing him with a departing nose lick.

"Looks like you're leaving us again, boy," Rosie says, not bothering to hide her disappointment. "I'm certain you'll find what you're looking for. I can *feel* it."

Shadow and I make our way off the porch and down the white pebble path.

"Goodbye," I call over my shoulder when we reach the street. "And thank you."

Shadow follows my lead and barks his farewell.

Rosie and George leave the old dog to rest on his blanket. Not entirely sure about what to make of the situation, they follow us until they reach the end of their path, where George is left scratching his head. "Should we stop him?" he asks Rosie.

"I don't think we could if we tried," Rosie replies, waving after us. "Whatever they're looking for, we're obviously not it."

Rosie waves until we disappear around the bend of their street, and as the first stars twinkle in a clear night sky, our hearts are light and at peace.

14

Lost

An entire night and day later, with only a few short hours of rest since leaving Rosie and George's house, we stumble through the last fingers of another golden afternoon's sunlight.

Shadow's tired, but true to his cattle-dog breed, he's persistent. He keeps himself alert, seeing every twitch in the grass before I do and pinpointing the source of every noise first as well, even ones I should be the most familiar with, like the rumble of an oncoming engine.

We hear it coming from the other side of a crest we ourselves conquered only moments ago. It's too loud to be a car: perhaps a tractor, or some other form of farm vehicle. There's not much else I'd expect to encounter on such a quiet country road.

I don't want Shadow to be seen. Rosie and George wanting to take him to have his microchip scanned reminded me of just how quickly he could end up back at Claire's. I can't risk that, so I quickly usher him away from the road and back into the grass where we wait for whatever it is to pass us by.

The rumble grows louder. It sounds huge.

We glue our eyes to the top of the crest, and as the sparkling silver tips of twin exhaust stacks jut into the air, I know exactly what is headed our way. Something I never wanted to see again in such close proximity - a truck.

"Don't move!" I command Shadow. I know we are far enough from the road to not be in any danger, but the niggle of fear that the memory of my accident induces is stronger than logic.

Although Shadow didn't look as though he had any intention of moving before my command, my harsh tone freezes him to the point where he almost dares not to breathe.

The exhaust stacks loom higher over the rise. The crunch of a downward changing gear makes the engine grumble louder and forces two puffs of black smoke up out of the stacks. It reminds me of two angry dragons sending out a warning that they're about to breathe fire.

Before long, the rest of the truck climbs into view. It's intimidating, to say the least: blacker than the darkest night, with a giant silver grille across the front that could easily open up to a furnace where a witch might roast little children alive.

I don't like anything about it.

The frame splitting the windscreen into two halves makes the truck appear to have eyes, while the glare reflecting off those two eyes feels as though it's hiding the kind of driver who would steer to hit instead of miss.

Altogether the truck conjures up a memory far worse than that of my accident. It's exactly the kind of thing those two grotesque neighbours of Claire's might drive. And it's slowing down!

That's not possible, I think. There's no way they could have seen Shadow from back there!

The truck slows further, sending my niggle of fear into overdrive. Before it can roll an inch closer, my finger's pointed to the ground and I hear myself shouting, "Down, Shadow! Get down *now*!"

Shadow buries himself so deep in the grass that even I struggle to find him. I've no doubt he sees the memory of Greg and Sam replaying in my head, something neither of us are willing to risk a repeat of.

"Don't move!" I warn as the truck slows even further. I still can't believe the driver could possibly have spotted Shadow, but as if following a tracking collar, the truck idles to a stop in the worst place possible – right next to where he hides in the grass.

The truck rattles, hisses, and eventually falls silent.

Minutes pass without any movement from inside.

What are they doing, I wonder? I know it's irrational to believe it could possibly be Greg and Sam, and the longer I study the truck, the more I notice the way its metallic-black paintwork is polished to a mirror-like shine. There's not a splatter of bug guts anywhere on the windscreen and the furnace-like grille glistens like my great grandmother's favourite cutlery set. If it were Greg and Sam sitting in there, the outside of the truck would tell an entirely different story.

"Maybe it's broken down," I say to Shadow, who peeks

up from between the grass as if to ask does that mean I can breathe again.

"Just wait. Stay there," I say, this time calmly enough for him to understand it as more of a precaution.

After a few more minutes of anxious silence, the driver's door finally swings open.

The first thing I see is a pair of feet clad in water-ski sized thongs, just like the ones Greg and Sam wore. Instantly my heart flies up into my throat. "Oh no, Shadow."

Shadow cowers anew without needing a further command.

Two legs stretch down from the cab. They're longer and skinnier than I remember. Still a bit hairy, definitely male, but unless either Greg or Sam has lost a ton of weight in the last couple of days, I think I can allow Shadow to breathe again.

The rest of the driver slides into view, and as his feet slap down against the bitumen, I can confirm, "It's ok, Shadow. It's definitely not them."

Shadow untangles himself from his hiding spot. He scratches away a couple of grass seeds stuck to his neck and then creeps up beside me for his own glimpse at the driver.

Looking not much older than me, with a mop of wild caramel hair that could possibly have been trimmed by a mate as a dare, the driver pulls a phone from the pocket of a checkered shirt that belongs on top of a horse instead of smiley-face-patterned board shorts. He holds the phone up to the sky like an antenna and begins to zigzag his way across the road behind it.

"He looks lost," I say to Shadow. "He also looks way too

young to be driving that thing. Don't you have to be, like, thirty to get a truck license?"

The truck driver covers the entire width of the road twice while fixated on his phone. "Damn GPS!" I hear him mumble.

"Maybe he stole it." I continue with my guessing game. "I mean shouldn't he be wearing a uniform or something?"

His search for service leads him closer to Shadow and I. He follows the bars on his phone all the way off the bitumen and into the grass where he finally stops with an "Ooh! Got ya!" He's so close to Shadow, he would only need to look down to see him.

Too preoccupied with his phone to notice anything else, the driver starts talking into it as though it doesn't understand English. "Di...rec...tions to Syd...ney."

His request peaks my interest. Sydney! It's not Echuca, but it's south! And I'm certain it's a lot closer to Astrid than where we are now. I wonder how hard it would be to hitch a ride?

I glance over the trailer. It's four closed-in high walls offer no gaps at all for Shadow to sneak into. The only way would be in the actual truck, with a driver who's possibly a thief, and who we don't know at all.

While the driver repeats his request for directions to Sydney, I begin to scrutinise him. I know it's not the best - or safest - way to judge someone, but right now, I haven't got much else to go on.

It's a bit of a risk, but this stranger on the side of the road might just be our quickest way to Astrid.

15

The driver

The first thing I notice about the driver is that even though he's as frustrated as anything with his phone, his eyes remain calm. There's something deeply placid about them, like a wisdom that would usually accompany a face full of wrinkles. They're kind, like Rosie's – the same sort of washed-out hazel colour too – and warm, like they wouldn't know what a sarcastic glare was.

The tiny creases around them prove he squints a lot. It might be from the sun, but the way his lips curl up, instead of down at the corners, hint toward someone who's no stranger to a smile.

He's tall enough that a girl of my height would probably have to stand on tippy-toes to kiss him – a thought that stupidly makes me blush – and he's thin. Not skinny, but more - wiry. Strong looking, like the kind of strong you get from hard work rather than the gym.

Overall, the warm eyes, the smile creases, the curled-up lips, and the mismatched outfit that points a long way away from excessive vanity, makes me think he might be sympathetic to a lost dog, but that could also be a problem. He might take Shadow to a vet, which will lead us straight back to Claire.

Giving up on trying to get directions out of his phone, he starts talking to himself. "You'd think I'd know this area by now. Hope I can turn around down there somewhere."

He sounds like he might have steered himself wrong one too many times before.

He tries to see an end to the road ahead. "The boss is gunna kill me if I don't get to Sydney on time. Bugger!"

He picks his way back out of the grass. "Well, it'll be what it'll be, I suppose."

Starting back toward his truck, which I can no longer assume to be stolen, he leaves me with my own decision, and one I don't have much time to make. Do I let Shadow show himself and try to hitch a ride, or do I let the driver go and make Shadow walk – all the way to Echuca, wherever in the world that may be.

Shadow's now scratching another grass seed from the side of his belly.

"What do you think?" I ask him, knowing the question is pointless; he'll do whatever I think is best.

Shadow forgets the grass seed and looks up at me.

"Well?" I push, hoping for some kind of answer.

He stands up, raises his nose toward the driver for a second, and then loud enough to be heard all the way down the street, Shadow barks.

My first reaction is to shoosh him. I know I wanted an answer, but something a little more subtle might have been nice.

The driver, of course, hears Shadow's bark. He stops just shy of pulling himself back up into his truck and turns to inspect the grass where the noise came from. He doesn't see anything at first; even standing, Shadow is too well hidden.

The curiosity he shows interests me. It's more than just 'I wonder what that was,' it's concerned, like he's already jumped to the conclusion the bark he heard was a cry for help, like there's no way he's leaving without first making sure everything here is ok. It puts me a little more at ease, and Shadow obviously too, because before I can stop him, he steps forward and puts himself straight into the driver's view.

"Oh, there you are," the drivers says, as if he only just lost Shadow five minutes ago.

Without needing anyone to explain to him that at full height he might come across as a bit intimidating to a strange dog, he folds himself into a squat, stretches one hand out, palm side down to show he's not about to strike or grab, and quietly soothes, "Hey, little buddy. It's alright."

His actions put him straight into the 'animal person' category which, in my opinion, any other animal person can pick a mile away.

"It's ok," I tell Shadow, who has decided to wait for my blessing before taking the final steps toward the outstretched hand.

Noticing Shadow's indecision, the driver tells him, "Hang on, I've got something in the truck. You hungry?"

He stands up slowly, so as not to frighten, climbs into his truck and returns with a plastic-wrapped sandwich. "It's not *fresh* fresh," he says, tearing off a chunk, "but it's been in the fridge in the truck, so it's still good."

Shadow glances at me for confirmation. I wouldn't usually let him take food from strangers by the side of the road, but these aren't usual times. Plus, with the driver becoming more and more endearing by the second, I would almost feel bad for him if Shadow turned his nose up at his offer of help.

I give Shadow the nod and he quickly snatches the chunk before taking a step back to scoff it down.

"Did you even chew that?" The driver laughs, offering a second, and then a third chunk.

"There you go, mate. Where you headed then? You look just as lost as me."

Shadow finishes his meal a little too quickly and follows it through with a closed-mouth burp.

"You must be lost," the driver decides. "As hungry as that! And there's nothing around here for miles. I should know. I took a wrong turn before the highway back at Damper Creek there. I've been on this road for ages now."

Standing up again, he shields his eyes from the setting sun and takes in the vastness of the area.

"You're not gunna do too well out here alone, that's for sure. Plus a good-looking bluey like you can get picked up by the wrong person, if you know what I mean? I'll tell you what. I'm headed for Sydney – if I can find my way back to the highway, that is – and I'm in a bit of a hurry to be honest, so I can't really do much about getting you home today. But if you wanna come for a drive, I could use the company. I'll be back up this way again in a couple of days. We can see where you come from then, huh?"

"Yes, Shadow," I say, now fully smitten. "That's perfect! We'll go with him."

Shadow relays my yes with a boisterous wag of his tail and the same high-pitched bark he would give when asked if he wants to go for a run.

The driver allows a surprised smile to push his cheeks up until his eyes squint. The creases around them deepen and prove my theory. He definitely does that a lot.

"If I didn't know any better," he then says, "I'd almost think you just said *yes.*"

After obtaining a quick once over to check that he isn't hurt in any way, Shadow follows the driver around to the passenger side and allows himself to be effortlessly lifted up onto the seat. I slot myself in beside him while the driver jogs around and climbs up into his side of the truck.

The engine rattles to life and shortly after, the huge wheels beneath us roll into motion.

"Comfy?" The driver asks Shadow a moment later.

Shadow answers with a bark so vigorous, it lifts parts of him off his seat.

With a nod, as though that was the exact answer he expected, the driver turns back to his windscreen. "Righteo, then, let's see if we can find somewhere to turn around, hey?"

16

One so right

One impressively tight U-turn later, the driver finds his way back to the highway. He then pushes his truck through more gears than I thought existed and grafts himself deep into his seat for the long drive ahead.

Shadow currently couldn't care less about our direction of travel. He's enthroned himself in his own high-backed, air-cushioned seat like a king on a VIP tour. I half expect him to reach over and tap the driver on the shoulder, point his other paw toward the windscreen and in a royal British accent say, 'You there. What's that over there?'

He holds his regal sightseeing position for hours, until the moon has arced halfway across the sky and the towns we fly through become lost under a late-night blanket of darkness. With nothing of interest left to look at in the outside world, he shuffles his upright body sideways toward the driver and eyeballs him with the hope of being further entertained.

The driver notices the intensity with which he is now being watched. He shifts his eyes sideways toward Shadow and at the same time curls the ends of his lips up. "What?" he quizzes. "Why are you staring?"

Shadow brushes the seat clean with his tail. He opens his mouth and snuffs out a throaty grunt as if he wants to answer, but doesn't quite know which bark to use.

The driver's half-smile widens. "Are you bored? Is that what the staring's all about?"

Shadow grunts again. He likes this game.

"I'll take that as a yes. Alright then. Well, since we've got a whole lot of time and not a whole lot for you to do, um, let's get acquainted, shall we?"

Shadow's mouth closes and his head angles left. He's heard the tone of the question, but none of the words match any he knows.

"Acquainted!" The driver seems to be getting used to Shadow's level of engagement. "You know, get to know each other?"

Shadow's head tips further to the side: nope, don't know that one.

"Ok then," the driver reads Shadow like a book, "I'll start. I'm Mick and, let's see. I grew up on Mum and Dad's cattle farm out west of Rockhampton, at Wowan. You heard of it?"

He's starting to look at Shadow more expectantly than he probably should.

Shadow disappoints though. The driver, to whom I can finally put the name Mick, has him stumped.

"Guess not." Mick seems unfazed. "I'm not surprised; it's a little country town pretty far out in the sticks. Um, been driving trucks on the farm since before I could walk pretty much. I was supposed to take it over one day, but the drought got too bad early last year. Heaps of cattle died; too many, you know? Mum and Dad had to walk away from the whole thing. They couldn't afford to stay."

He pauses for a second, presumably lost in the memory of the farm.

"Then they decided they were a bit too old to start something new." He forces himself to sound a little more upbeat. "So they retired. Mum was forty-three when she had me, and I'm twenty-two now, so, yeh, can't blame 'em really. They moved up north to Tully." He hits Shadow with a far less expectant look than the last time. "Don't suppose you know Tully? It's only about a hundred or so k's up the road from where I found you."

"We do!" I butt in, stealing Shadow's attention. "Rosie and George, Shadow. Maybe he knows them."

Shadow sees the same vision of the old couple as I do; firstly, George in spandex. It's something we never actually saw, but for some reason, it's the one image of him that stuck. Rosie's image is one containing gym clothes, desert roses and washed-out hazel eyes full of warmth. The same warmth I first saw in Mick's...washed-out...hazel – hang on!

Mick starts talking again. He's saying something about how his dad's mate gave him his current job, but I've stopped listening. I can see his lips moving, but the words aren't filtering through properly. Rosie mentioned a farm; Mick's parents had a farm. If she was forty-three when she had him, she fits the bill; she looked to be in her mid-sixties. Plus the more he talks, the more I hear both Rosie and George in his voice. I thought it sounded familiar for some reason. To top it all off, their son was called Michael, which I'm pretty certain is the long version of Mick. I bet it's him! I bet he's their son! If so, what a coincidence. Unless...it's not?

I remember Rosie saying some things happen for a reason. I wonder if, for some reason we don't yet know, we were meant to meet Mick. We didn't stay to meet him at the house, like she wanted us to, and he didn't stop in anyway. Then he got himself lost and pulled up at the exact spot Shadow and I stood.

There must be a reason. There has to be. But what?

***

I can't stop staring at Mick. I can't stop wondering if we were supposed to meet him or if it was just a coincidence. I keep waiting for him to say something that will give me an aha moment. Something like I met this dream girl online called Astrid, but then the connection died and I lost her. I wish I knew someone who knew her.

He doesn't say anything though. He's been quietly listening to the radio since Shadow didn't offer up his own life story, and he's been yawning - a lot!

Through one of his yawns, so wide it could almost swallow the steering wheel, he points out an upcoming truck stop sign to Shadow and asks, "You hungry there, mate?"

Shadow's lying down again. His paws are dangling over the front of his seat and his head's flopped over the side facing Mick. He's been slipping in and out of a doze since his and Mick's one-sided conversation ended, but the word 'hungry' brings him bolt upright.

Mick's gaping yawn ends in laughter. "At ease, soldier!" He jokes. "Five minutes, mate. We'll be there in five minutes."

Soon enough, the glow from the sign-posted Ilbilbie truck stop breaks the otherwise pitch-black ahead. Nestled in the middle of a rural nowhere, it's a welcoming contrast to the dark, and one that sends a ripple of relief through both Mick and Shadow.

A turn of a key and the loud hiss of the parking brake leaves the truck in cool-down mode. Mick pushes his door open and shivers as the unexpectedly cool midnight air sneaks its way into the cab. "Oh man, I'm busting!" he fills Shadow in. "You need to go too?"

He climbs down, calls Shadow across to the driver's seat, then carefully lifts him out and places him squarely on the ground. "There's twenty-two wheels there for you to choose from, mate," he points out. "Take your pick."

Shadow's already taken such a liking to Mick that he chooses the wheel right beside him, forcing me to awkwardly look away. I hum to myself to block out the sound of tinkling, but can't not hear Mick's ridiculously long sigh of relief, and the wit in his voice when he's done. "Thank God for tires, hey, mate?"

How lucky are we? I think to myself. We could have been picked up by a million wrong people, but we found someone so right. How lucky are we!

17

Memories and dreams

In a deserted outdoor eating area lit only by a sign boasting low fuel prices and the best meals for miles, a lone picnic table looks like it could use some company.

Shadow and I park ourselves like hens on the bench seat behind, while Mick proves an old-school upbringing by saying, "I'll be two shakes of a lamb's tail. I'll order us some dinner. Stay!"

Aside from the quiet hum of a padlocked ice freezer, the truck stop is surrounded in a peaceful late-night calm. There are only two trucks, besides Mick's, resting silently in the dark of the gravel parking bay. There's no sound from the nearby highway, and with the only movement being the flickering of the restaurant's neon blue 'open' sign, it's easy to imagine we've stepped out of the truck and into the first episode of *Life After People*.

Mick returns, a little longer than the promised lamb's tail time-frame, but still relatively quickly.

I watched him as he rushed inside. He spun around every other second while ordering to check that Shadow hadn't moved. I can imagine he would have been back out in a flash if he'd thought it was necessary.

He breaks into a full body stretch and gazes around. "It's like one of those movies where everyone's disappeared" he says, voicing my exact thoughts. "Lucky Mrs. Shingle's still here. I ordered steak burgers. You eat steak burgers, mate?"

Shadow one hundred percent understands the word steak and doesn't hold back in showing that it's on an endless list of his favourite things.

It isn't long before the delicious aromas of sizzling steak and melting cheese escape the heat of the greasy kitchen, leaving Shadow not only licking his lips in anticipation, but also shuffling repeatedly back and forth between Mick and I, searching our empty hands with confusion.

"It's coming," I tell him every couple of minutes. "Be patient."

Mick kicks his long legs out under the wooden table and wraps the thin flannelette shirt he threw on, before getting out of the truck, tight across his chest. "Never been a fan of the cold," he says, taking one hand and running it upward along Shadow's back, watching the thick hairs stand up and sift through his splayed fingers. "Don't suppose that's an issue for you though, huh?"

He nods in the direction of a street sign on the opposite side of the highway. It's barely visible in the dark and I wouldn't have noticed it at all if he didn't point it out. "I wanna buy a place somewhere down there one day," he says dreamily. "Perfect weather here, I reckon. Not too cold, not too hot. You wouldn't think it, but the beach is only about ten k's down that road. There's this really tiny town at the end called Cape Point. I left the trailer here once and went down to have a look, out of curiosity. It's really quiet and beautiful: my kind of place – away from too many people, bush and beach all in one. I'll get a dog, just like you hopefully. Maybe meet some gorgeous girl who likes horses. We can ride along the beach together and——"

He pulls himself up as the lights from a car turn into the truck stop. It parks next to the fuel bowsers, where a family of four with tired faces proving they've travelled a lot further than us, get out.

The father fills the car up while the mum and her two daughters head toward the shop. One of the girls is around my age. Tall and skinny as well, with blonde, curly hair not much shorter than mine.

The sight of her has Mick catching his breath.

Maybe I'm his type. I think to myself, feeling a little bit chuffed.

He watches her until she disappears inside, and when he speaks again, he sounds less like the cheerful Mick we've been traveling with all day, and more like the kind of Mick that Rosie seemed so worried about. "Who am I to dream."

It might be nothing more than the floodlight shining on the clear of Mick's eyes, but it almost looks like he's tearing up. I can't imagine why he wouldn't think himself worthy of dreaming or perhaps worthy of finding a nice girl. Maybe it's to do with the loss of the family farm. Maybe it's left him feeling like a failure.

Still watching for the girl's return, he lays his arm over Shadow's back and absentmindedly strokes his fur.

Feeling for what he and his family must have gone

through, I place my hand over Mick's and imagine I can feel the rounds of his knuckles through the browned skin.

He abandons his watch to look down at his hand and a hint of confusion crosses his face. "It's the strangest thing," he says to Shadow. "Back there on the road today, it was almost like you...*wanted* to come with me. And when I talk, it feels like you're actually listening. I mean, I know you don't understand what I'm saying, but it feels like I'm being heard."

"You must have been on the road too long, Mick." A short, full-figured woman lightens the mood with a voice like a rasp and two full plates. "Talking to the animals now, huh? Have to start calling you Dr Doolittle. Who's your little friend then?"

"Not exactly sure," Mick replies without the slightest trace of embarrassment. "Picked him up after I took a wrong turn up north today. Wasn't a house around for miles and he practically begged me to take him. I've got a few days off when I get back from Sydney. I'll drive back up there then and see if I can find where he came from."

"Sounds like a lot of hard work. Just put a post on social media. My kids do that sort of stuff all the time."

Mick smirks at the suggestion, "Do I look social to you?"

"Oh, come on, Mick. I thought everyone your age was into that sort of stuff. Surprised you haven't already taken a selfie with him, or a photo of your food, to be honest."

"Seriously? I've been stopping here for how many months now? Like ten or so? When have you ever seen me take a selfie?"

"Do you want me to take one? You look so cute together,

all huddled up with your arm around him. Surely you've got a friend who can post it for you? Who knows, the owner might be a pretty little thing who sees it and thinks, oooohhh, I get my dog back *and* a nice man."

Mick is now grinning from ear to ear and practically glowing red with embarrassment.

"You're a nutter," he teases bashfully, and I have to silently thank the woman for lifting his spirits. "Can we have our dinner now?" he pleads as over-dramatically as possible.

Shadow, interested in none of the conversation whatsoever, has removed himself from under Mick's arm and sits with thumping tail, watching the woman's plated hands as they accentuate her words.

"You won't let him eat off the plate, will you?" she says, forgetting all about the photo opportunity and switching to a motherly tone. "I'll have to throw it out if you do."

"I'll *hand feed* him, unless of course you've got a spare knife and fork?"

After the woman leaves, Mick fills Shadow in. "That was old Mrs. Shingle."

He pushes one of the plates over with a cheeky smile. "Go on, dig in. Your germs'll wash off just as easily as mine."

Shadow and Mick take to their mounded burgers with enthusiasm. While Mick manages to let only a few shreds of lettuce slip to his lap, Shadow struggles to keep more than that on his plate. I watch him chase the burger with his nose until it has visited every inch of the plate and most of the surrounding table, leaving a sticky trail of tomato sauce in its wake.

Mick lets out a hearty laugh as the cat and mouse game comes to an abrupt end with a soggy slap directly on his right foot. He works his upper half under the table to pry the ingredients from between his toes. "Crikey, mate, and I thought *my* table manners were bad."

Shadow springs from the bench seat to aid the clean-up and it isn't long before he has proudly eliminated any sign that he has dined here tonight. With another cheeky egg-on from Mick, he then allocates himself as dishwasher.

"Look at that," Mick praises afterwards, holding his tongue-washed plate out like a trophy. "Old Mrs. Shingle will probably stack that straight back in the rack for the next person." A new bout of laughter escapes his mouth and fills the cool night air, and for a moment I forget all about the circumstances under which we are here. I forget the direction in which we are headed and the obstacles we have yet to face. I forget that there is anything beyond this beautiful and most peaceful of moments: at a deserted truck stop in the middle of nowhere, a man and his dog enjoying the simplest of life's pleasures together.

Then there's me. I am still here... and that is why we must continue.

18

Coincidence

After a precisely timed and well-earned eight-hour rest, Mick, Shadow, and I are once again rolling our way through the ever-changing early morning landscape, on route to the hustle and bustle of industrial Sydney.

According to Mick, we still have a staggering seventeen hours to sit through when his phone rings and he presses it straight to loudspeaker. "I'm just about through Rocky, boss," Mick says, as if he knows exactly why he's getting the call. "Don't worry, I won't be late."

The man at the other end sounds like he's already made a hundred business calls today and has no time left for small talk. "I need you to make a deviation and pick up a couple of pallets from the yard in Surfers Paradise. Actually, sorry, but it might be an overnighter, the show's on down there."

"Are you kidding?" Mick's not pleased. "If the shows on, I'll be lucky to even get *in* there! I'm supposed to be having a few days off after Sydney, remember?" He glances at Shadow. "Plus I've kind of got something I need to do, sooner rather than later, when I get back."

"Don't worry, Mick, you'll still get your days off. You've earned 'em fair and square, mate." He slows down enough to take on a more caring tone. "How, ah...how are you doing anyway?"

The question seems to be aimed at something more than Mick's general wellbeing, but Mick ignores its specific nature and brushes his boss's concern off with a hasty, "Better than ever."

"Ok. Good to hear." His boss couldn't sound less convinced if he tried. "I'll tell you what. I'll shuffle some things around, and throw in a couple extra days on top, so you can do whatever it is you need to do when you get back to Rocky. How's that sound?"

"Yeh, that'd be great, boss. Thanks heaps."

After hanging up, Mick turns to Shadow. "Well, my little travel buddy, looks like you're stuck with me for a bit longer than expected."

***

The first few hundred kilometres after Rockhampton, or Rocky, as Mick called it, aren't anything I'd write home about.

The road is mostly flat, with long straights, a gradual rise and fall every so often, and sweeping curves revealing nothing more than a continuation of the same monotonous landscape as before. The overall colour scheme has noticeably changed since Mick first picked Shadow and I up. The tropical greens have been replaced with sunburnt browns, lush is now withered, and the once thick, dark, rain clouds are now scarce, white, wispy, and unforgivingly dry.

Mick passes the time telling Shadow more about his old

life on the farm. His stories are littered with snippets of his parents. "Mum's always gotta look good, Dad's dry sense of humour, always teasing each other." Everything he says describes Rosie and George to a tee.

I know from Rosie that he didn't end up stopping in as she'd hoped, so I don't expect he knows they've already met Shadow. I wonder if there's a way we can tell him. Maybe he would then pick up the same vibes as Rosie. Maybe he might also feel my presence, more so than just the feeling of being listened to by Shadow.

He rambles on until Shadow nods off. Spending so much time talking about his parents has given him the urge to call them, and a minute later, he's on the phone again.

After a couple of rings, the exact voice I expected relays through the truck's speakers: Rosie's.

She sounds every bit as delightful as I remember and barely gets past, "Hello. How are you?" before jumping right into her news. "We got a new dog!"

"You did?" Mick's excitement rivals his Mum's. "When?"

"The other day when you were supposed to come over. Two, actually, but one left. The other one's still here. He's a beautiful old thing. I think your dad's fallen in love."

"Wait a sec, Mum; I'm not following. What do you mean, you got two, but one left? Why did you get two? Where did the other one go? Where did you get them from?"

"Hang on, I'll just make a cup of tea and then I'll tell you all about it. Here, talk to your dad for a minute."

George's voice crackles through the phone. "Michael?"

"Hi, Dad. Mum said you got a dog?"

"I'll let her tell you about it, but I'm just letting you know

now though, I think she's lost a couple of marbles, if you know what I mean."

"Why's that?"

"Hang on, she's back. No, I didn't tell him anything: finish making your tea. Oh, you don't want tea now. I won't tell him. Look, *I'll* make the tea. Michael, apparently I'll talk to you later, mate."

"Ok, Dad, I'll—— Oh, hi, Mum – again. Alright, tell me the dog story."

"Well..."

I listen to Rosie's detailed account of Shadow's and my visit. She tells Mick about the biscuit jar, the figurine, the old dog and all his protruding bones. She confirms what I had wondered about - he wasn't microchipped, wasn't missed by anyone.

As she gets closer to the part about how she believed to know Shadow's name, I hear George in the background: "That's enough now, dear."

"Ignore him." Rosie pushes on. "Anyway, the other dog, the one that left...oh, did I tell you what type of dog it was yet?"

"Not yet."

"Oh. So it was a cattle dog. It looked a bit like Luna from the farm."

"Oh really?" Mick gets in before Rosie can continue. "I found a cattle dog yesterday too." He glances at Shadow, who's once again wide awake and pricking his ears between voices. "Come to think of it, this one looks a bit like Luna too."

Rosie falls silent long enough for me to picture her putting two and two together.

George calls out from the background again, "Coincidence, dear. Nothing more."

Rosie's not buying it. "It wouldn't, by chance, have a white diamond of hair between its ears and one ear a bit bent over at the top, would it? And it looks like it's wearing a sort of heart-shaped mask?"

Mick's brows almost meet as he gives Shadow a more thorough eyeing-off. "Ah, yeh, actually, he does. How'd you...what? You don't think it's the same dog, do you?"

"Where did you find him?"

"About a hundred k's down the road from your place. I got lost and ended up on this back road. I stopped to get reception and he kind of just walked out of the grass, like he——"

"Like he knew what he was doing?" Rosie finishes Mick's sentence.

"Well, yeh, sort of like that. A lot like that actually. What made you say that?"

"Oh, Michael!" Rosie sounds like she's just found the only key to a secret garden. "It has to be the same one. That dog is truly something special. He has an——"

I hear George abruptly start coughing, drowning Rosie out.

"Is dad alright?" Mick asks. "What were you about to say, Mum? He has a what?"

George coughs again, louder and quite obviously staged. His voice rings of warning when he says, "Rosie, can I——?"

The phone sounds as though someone's placed their hand

over it and only incoherent, muffled whispers break through.

"What's going on?" Mick wants to know. "What are you guys whispering about? Mum? What does the dog have?"

The hand is removed and George takes over the conversation. "He has an excellent owner somewhere. That's what your mum was about to say. He's something special because of how well trained he is. That's all, mate."

Mick isn't convinced. "So what was all the whispering about?"

"You know what your mum's like, mate. She likes to think everything happens for a reason. She doesn't think it's a coincidence that you found the same dog that was here. But, in reality, a hundred k's isn't unheard of for a dog to travel in a few days. I wouldn't go reading too much into it."

"Yeh." Mick hesitates. "I suppose. Still, Mum's right; it is pretty coincidental, don't you think?"

"Just a very lucky dog to have been picked up by the right person. That's what I think."

After hanging up, Mick spends a second or two gawking at Shadow. "How crazy is that?"

He turns back to the road and loses himself in thought. "Very coincidental indeed."

***

Mick's conversation with his parents is clearly playing on his mind. Every now and then he switches his attention over to Shadow for a few seconds, and each time he does, he rattles off a new question that I'd love to be able to give him the answer to: "How far did you walk before Mum and Dad's place? They said you weren't from around there. Why did you leave? Where did you find the other dog? How weird is it that I, of all people, found you? I wonder if it is just a coincidence. Where are you from then?"

Shadow listens to each question intently. I try my best to translate through pictures, but with my own thoughts too preoccupied, there's not a lot getting through to him.

Why did George not let Rosie tell the whole story, is what *I'm* wondering about. Why did he stop her? I'm certain she was about to say he has an angel. She could have given Mick Shadow's name! Why wouldn't he let her? If she could have told Mick about me, maybe he would have started to feel my presence, just like she did. Maybe over time, I could have found a way to communicate where we are trying to go. Maybe he could have taken us the whole way. Maybe, as Rosie said, some things happen for a reason; in which case, I guess, *also* for a reason, maybe some things don't.

19

The backpackers

Last night's cool air is nowhere to be seen. The world outside is a melting pot of bitumen and burnt grass. Heat waves turn the road ahead into a shimmering mass while the trees droop so low they almost brush the top of Mick's truck.

I'm still stuck in my thoughts. Mick seems to be also, and Shadow's gone back to snoozing, when halfway up a long, steep rise, the voice from a passing truck's driver blurts through Mick's UHF radio. "Copy there, southbound? Take it easy at the top there, mate; there's a break down on the other side."

Mick eases cautiously off the accelerator before responding. "Cheers, mate, I'll check it out."

True to the warning, as we reach the top of the rise, Mick is forced to swerve into the opposite lane for a mini van parked precariously on the white line of the downward run. The mini van's back right tire is completely flat. Nobody's thought to turn on the caution lights and the two people scratching their heads beside it are clearly oblivious to the dangers of standing so far out on the road.

The male half is holding a car jack like it's an object from another planet. Mick's noticed the cluelessness of the couple as well. "Doesn't look like they're going anywhere in a hurry," he says. "Someone really needs to tell them to get off the road though." He turns to Shadow. "Don't you think?"

Shadow's nose is pressed hard against his window. He's watching the couple with the utmost fascination, not listening to Mick at all.

I feel like we really should help them. They don't look much older than me, and Mick's right; they definitely shouldn't be standing so far out on the road like that. I pull Shadow away from the window. "Hey, see if you can get Mick to stop. Speak, Shadow. Speak!"

Shadow's snappy bark and his immediate head spin back toward his window, makes Mick laugh. "Already on it, mate," he says. "Just gotta find somewhere to pull over."

About half a kilometre further along, Mick finds a flat run long enough to fit his entire truck. He hesitates before lifting Shadow out. "Now listen," he chooses his sternest tone, "I can't leave you in here. It'll get too hot. But you have to stay right beside me. You understand heel?"

"You have to listen to him, Shadow," I say, every bit as stern as Mick. "We're right beside the highway here. You really can't give him any reason to worry. Understood?"

Shadow understands perfectly. He quickly eliminates his usual smile, sits up soldier straight, and dips his nose down to offer Mick his strictest display of obedience.

"Ok." Mick carries Shadow to the ground. He leaves one hand resting over his back, shuffles half a step forward, and tests Shadow's obedience, "Heel."

"Stay right beside him," I translate, knowing Shadow's never actually been taught the word heel.

Shadow obeys to the centimetre. One step forward, stop.

Mick tests his luck with a second step, followed by another, "Heel." Shadow doesn't disappoint.

Growing more confident with each step, Mick repeats the command three more times before, thoroughly impressed, praising Shadow. "Mum and Dad weren't lying. You are well trained."

We are still a way off the mini van, but already the two strandees come rushing toward us, glistening in more sweat than seems appropriate, even for the current heat. At first glance, the girl reminds me of Astrid's old horse, Taffy. She's just as sleek, with the same proud trot, and her show-shined ponytail of strawberry blonde hair kicks up at the ends with each step, just like Taffy's used to. The guy loping beside her looks a little worse for wear. He's already stumbled over his own feet twice and he's brandishing the car jack out in front of a shirtless upper half that could stand to do a few sit-ups.

He's out of breath by the time he reaches us. It doesn't stop his smile though. It looks like it's been plastered to his face for the same amount of days that his bloodshot eyes have been awake. It makes me wonder what kind of fumes, from what kind of party, his body might be running on.

He coughs up at least one lung before catching his breath enough to stand up straight.

"Sank you," he wheezes, sounding a lot like my grade nine German teacher, while presenting the car jack to Mick like an offering. He instantly corrects himself. "Sorry, I have meant, *th*-ank you. I am still practicing."

Mick offers an introductory smile that compels the girl to an abrupt halt a few steps shy. She attempts a quick neatening pat down of her white crop top and high-waisted cut-off shorts.

Satisfied with herself, she nudges her way past her companion and throws one hand demurely toward Mick. "Mila," she states proudly, showing off a perfect row of staggeringly white teeth. "And this is my brother, Nico." She waves carelessly to the side. "We are traveling from Germany. Our tire is flat."

Before Mick has a chance to accept Mila's hand, Nico shoves the jack in its place and beams expectantly. "You can fix?"

Mila's lightly freckled peach face tries it's hardest to wrinkle. "You need to speak better English, Nico," she mothers, far less accented than her brother. "It's *can you* fix."

"Yeh, mate." Mick nods. "I should be able to help, if you've got a spare."

"Spare?" Nico's face drops below his comprehension. "We have only one of these." The grin returns. "You can fix, *ja?*"

Mila sticks almost closer to Mick's side than Shadow as he leads the way to the mini van's rear tire. On closer inspection, it's not only flat, but completely shredded.

Nico bends in and points to the tire, as if it's lack of air and jutting strands of canvas aren't indication enough. "Flat!" He feels the need to explain. He straightens himself up to recap the moment of explosion with a dramatic hand charade. "Boom! Big boom!

"Wow!" Mick makes a point of Nico's dramatisation. "That big, huh? How'd you survive that?"

"And there's George," I say to Shadow, who's so focused on waiting for Mick's next heel that my voice makes him jump. "Ooooh! I'm sorry," I joke. "Did you forget I was here already?"

Shadow ears flatten with guilt. But you told me to obey, the rapid flutter of his tail says.

"I'm just kidding." I give him a rub.

He's so relieved, he wriggles out from under my hand and jumps up on his hind legs for a hug. Mila, who was standing right behind me, steps forward at the same time as Shadow's front paws close in on my stomach. I bend down to give him a kiss, and as I do, I realise mine aren't the only arms wrapped around him. Oh my god! Mila just stepped right through me.

"Oooohh!" she squeals, believing Shadow has taken it upon himself to jump up on her for no reason. "Your puppy likes me. Look! Look! He wants to make friends. What is his name?"

Being stepped through feels just a bit too weird: not physically, more an invasion of personal space weird. I can't slip out of there quick enough, and as soon as I do, Shadow realises he's now jumping up on, and being hugged by a total stranger.

The face he makes is hilarious. He drops back to the ground quicker than I can say, "Down, Shadow," and takes Mila's excitement with him.

"Oh!" She frowns. "I don't think he wants to be my friend anymore."

A little embarrassed, Mick calls Shadow back to his side with another "Heel!"

"Sorry about that," he then says. "He's not my...ah...Blue. His name's Blue."

"Gee, that's original." I have to laugh. "You hear that, Shadow? You're now the one millionth blue cattle dog to be named Blue."

Mila doesn't seem to have heard the name before and finds it reason enough to fall over Shadow with another hug. "He is a cow dog, *ja*?"

"Yeah." Mick smirks. "Something along those lines."

Mila unlatches herself from Shadow's neck to wrestle the back pocket of her teeny-tiny shorts for her phone. "I have seen a cow dog a couple of days ago." She makes it sound as though seeing two cattle-dogs in two days - in Australia – is practically unheard of. "On the street." She's getting more excited by the second. "I show you; I have taken a photo." She holds up the screen and points. "You see?"

Mick takes a look, more out of courtesy than interest. I know he'll want to hurry up and get the couple on the road again and get out of here, so when his brows crease and he snatches the phone from Mila, my interest peaks.

The photo takes me by complete surprise. It's Shadow! I think it's from the morning after we left Claire's.

Mick widens the image with his fingers. "Where did you take this?" he asks Mila. "I'm pretty sure it's Blue. Certain, in fact."

Mila shines. "It is your dog? Really? I take this photo at... Nico, what is the name of this town?"

Nico's drawn-out accentuation of Babinda makes me think he's trying to explain a place that a flock of sheep have visited. "Bah-been-da! I can remember this name," he proudly points to his head, "because I think to myself I been ta Bah-been-da. I have a good memory, *ja?*"

His desperation for reward earns him a "Bloody genius, mate," from Mick. "I'll have to remember that one myself."

Mick sinks back into the photo. He sounds like a kid who's just realised he can't keep a found toy when he says, "At least I know where to look for his owners now, I guess." A little disheartened, he hands the phone back to Mila, pushes the jack into the dust under the mini van, and gets to work on the tire.

Less than twenty minutes later, we make our way back to the truck through a plethora of increasingly better pronounced "th-ank yous" from Nico, and a not particularly subtle attempt to delay our leaving from Mila.

I think she's taken a bit of a shine to Mick. I can't exactly blame her; it's hard not to. I think Astrid would melt too if she met him.

Mick has to work his way around Mila to lift Shadow up onto the passenger seat. She's tucked herself in right beside the door, where her arched back and hand placement on Mick's shoulder is doing more than just alluding to the level of her interest. "We are driving to Gympie next." She says it like a suggestion. "Then we stop for dinner. Would you like to join us for some dinner?"

Mick's clearly not blind to her efforts. Strangely enough

though, given how pretty she is, he doesn't appear all that interested. "Look, I'd love to," he begins a little awkwardly, "but I've kinda gotta get going. Maybe some other time, yeh?"

"Aww, too bad." Mila pouts. "Do you have a girlfriend?"

Hurrying himself up, Mick rounds the front of the truck and climbs up into the driver's side. Mila's less than a step behind, eagerly waiting for an answer.

"Ah, no." Mick politely tries to shut his door without physically pushing her out of the road. "Look, I'm sorry, Mila." He pulls a little more persuasively on the door until it swings in and taps her on the back. "But I've really gotta get going."

Mila completely ignores Mick's hint. Like she's decided if he's single, then he's mine.

Rather than move away, she allows the door to push her closer to Mick. "Where are you driving to now?" she asks, using her squashed position as an excuse to press her chest against Mick's leg.

Mick's eyebrows fly up and he forces the corners of his mouth down so as not to encourage her with a smile. "Ah, Gold Coast." He meets Mila's eyes as bluntly as possible. "*If* I can get going, that is."

Mila's pout is back. She sighs, "Ok," before finally giving in and moving away. Her deflation stirs Mick's sympathy. "I'm really sorry," he apologises, fighting to keep his tone neutral. "I'll see you around, hey?"

As Mick shuts the door, I hear Mila call back to Nico, "He has invited us to the Gold Coast. Have you heard? He has said I see you around."

***

As soon as we are once again on the move, Mick turns to Shadow and grins. "How funny were they? That Nico fella was hilarious the way he couldn't stop smiling. And Mila? Wow! How pretty was she? But crikey, talk about desperate – and pushy. I could've been a murderer or anything." His eyes take on the same dreamy shine as they did when he spoke about riding a horse along the beach. "I'd rather find a girl where you just…like…I don't know…click. Like the second you see them, you say to yourself, "There she is." He looks at Shadow, "You know?"

Shadow's lack of understanding lends him the same confused look as me. Mick is truly different from any of the boys I knew from school. I can't see even one of them complaining about a pretty girl being *too desperate*. More likely, they would have taken advantage of her willingness and then boasted about it. Mick's attitude seems so different. I guess that's the forced, early maturity of his upbringing on the farm shining through. I wish there would have been boys around like that when I was still alive. Maybe I might have actually gone out with one. But while it might be too late for me, it's not too late for Astrid. What a shame they'll never meet, I think, wondering if there's a way, and then dismissing the idea. No, let it go. Mick knows about Babinda now; it's too risky.

I look over at Shadow. Just focus on getting one of them there. That's enough.

20

The Gold Coast

We follow the road until the dried grass and wilting trees turn orange in the afternoon sun, and then we follow it some more. We slow down through scuds of rain, speed up on brand new four-lane stretches of highway, slip through patches of rain forest, and pass a group of individual giant rock formations that Mick points out as "The Glass House Mountains." They're spectacularly out of place, jutting out of the grazing lands around them in all sorts of odd shapes. Almost like random chunks of whole mountains that have been stolen, brought here and carelessly dumped before the thieves could be caught.

We reach the city of Brisbane, crawl alongside a million other cars and trucks up a giant bridge over the muddiest river I can ever remember seeing, and as evening approaches, spot the roller coasters of Gold Coast theme parks I always dreamt of visiting as a child.

Mick starts to fidget as we finally turn off the highway. He follows a sign pointing east toward the Gold Coast's famous Surfers Paradise and for the first time in hours, turns the radio down enough to strike up a random conversation with Shadow.

"So I wonder what your name actually is." He must have been thinking about it ever since we left Mila and Nico. "I can't call you Blue. Every cattle dog is called Blue."

"About time he realised." I laugh.

He studies Shadow for name ideas. "We need something more original. I could call you Floppy because of your ear."

"Argh! Seriously, Mick? Shadow, cover your ear. Paw up!"

Shadow copies my hand movement and swipes a paw over his floppy-tipped ear.

"Look sad, Shadow. You don't want to be called Floppy, do you? Sad, Shadow, sad."

Mick's intrigued by Shadow's paw action and the shameful way he buries his nose in the seat. "How did you...? Do you understand ear? Floppy?"

Shadow pushes his nose deeper.

"Ok, ok. Wow! Um, how about – Diamond because of the white patch between your ears? No, that sounds like a girl's name. Shark? Your tail's got a white tip, like a white pointer. Shark's cool. Or Silver? Lots of silver hairs. Stocky? Grinner? What about a human name? You act like a human half the time. Smarter than some I've met too, just quietly. What about Bob? John? Bill? I know – Doug. But spelled D.U.G, get it? You're a dog? You dig? Dug?"

"You might as well bring your head out of the seat," I tell Shadow. "The names are only getting worse."

Mick's way happier with his suggestion than he should be.

"What do you think? We could add a Mr. to it. Mr. Dug. Yeh?"

I almost want to cover my own ears and bury my face in the seat with Shadow.

Shadow is getting confused. His head's back up and he's not sure if he should keep attempting to cover his ear. His paw makes a couple more swipes and then he pauses with it in the air, waiting for further direction.

Mick sees Shadow's raised paw. "You want to shake? Oooh! Mr. Shake! That's perfect."

"Oh boy!" My eyes roll so far back, they take my whole upper body with them.

Mick grabs Shadow's paw and Shadow seems thoroughly pleased with himself. "Well, how do you do, Mr. Shake?" Mick sounds like he needs a top hat and a moustache. "It's such an honour to meet you."

"That's a way better name than Blue," he mutters a moment later, as we slow down for the first of a string of traffic lights. He then shifts into a more upright and alert position. "Well, that's the end of the good run. Welcome to the Gold Coast."

***

Mick manoeuvres his semi trailer like a graceful giant through the early evening Gold Coast streets while Shadow and I absorb every inch of unfamiliar city that creeps past our passenger window. Compared to the highway's solitude, the atmosphere outside is a vibrant and uplifting buzz of lights, cars, and people of every description. We crawl past restaurants packed with alfresco diners who eat and chat beneath strings of fairy lights, and stop for pedestrians strolling contentedly with ice creams in hand.

Judging by the bare arms and short skirts on a group of girls piling into a taxi on our left, I'm guessing today's heat has hung around longer than expected. A pleasant change from last night's cool.

"Might be summer's last hoorah," Mick says, eyeing off the girls.

He rolls the windows down to test his prediction and as he does, a rush of balmy air sweeps into the cab, bringing with it all the commotion of the city streets, as well as a salty taste hinting at the nearness of the ocean.

"How nice is that?" Mick mimics Shadow and I as we lift our noses to suck in the atmosphere.

"I'm not the biggest fan of crowds," he continues, "but for some reason every time I come here, I kind of feel like getting out, going for a walk, and I don't know, getting amongst it all, instead of just driving through, you know?"

Shadow's too preoccupied sifting through passing scents to pay any attention, so Mick pulls in another deep breath, savours it for a moment, and then mocks himself by exhaling loudly and replying on Shadow's behalf. "Yeh, mate, yeh, I know exactly what you mean. Was just gunna say the same thing actually."

We continue our stop-start toward the Surfers Paradise skyline until Mick eventually indicates right for a driveway ahead and announces, "We're here!"

All three of us shuffle eagerly forward, only to be disappointed by a heavily padlocked gate with a pitch-black holding yard behind it.

Without hesitation, Mick reaches straight for his phone.

"I was just about to call you." Mick's boss wastes no time delivering an explanation. "The driver who was supposed to meet you there with the load got sick. I only just found out. He won't be there till late tomorrow afternoon. Look, you're out of logbook hours and you were gunna have to do an overnighter anyway. It'll just be a bit more of a late start, that's all. I'll put you up in a motel for the night. Get you out of the truck for a bit, hey? Why don't you go for a walk down to the beach, go to the show maybe? Treat it like a night off. Have a feed, some fairy floss, if you're so inclined. Have a hot shower, sleep in tomorrow. You know, enjoy yourself for once."

A few more profuse sorrys and a "You owe me big time" later, Mick hangs up.

"Well, I guess that's that," he says, reaching over and rubbing Shadow between the ears. "Don't suppose you're up for a walk?"

***

With no clear direction and an entire evening to kill, Mick leads Shadow and I on a winding path deep into the hype of Saturday night Surfers Paradise. After almost twelve hours in the truck, the leg stretch is welcomed by all, and although a delay, Mick seems grateful for the opportunity to make his wish come true and 'get amongst it all'.

Unable to wipe the country-boy awe from his face, he excuses his way through the crowded, inner-city streets. He tries to find the tops of the tallest buildings and bemuses himself with some of the outfits that make his mismatching checkered shirt, board shorts and thongs ensemble look like a hand-picked fashion statement. All the while, he keeps a close eye on Shadow.

Through the car fumes, perfumes, colognes and food aromas, the salty tang of ocean mist filters through with gathering strength. Desperate to see the beach again, something I know Shadow will also have greatly missed, I decide it's time to fire Mick as our aimless leader. "Want to go to the beach, Shadow?" I ask. "Beach?"

Shadow knows the word so well that given a pen and paper, I'm certain he could almost spell it. His tail fans wildly and he darts away from Mick to follow me.

"Don't forget Mick," I remind him, who's momentarily preoccupied with a window full of designer watches.

Keen to get moving, Shadow spins back toward Mick, races in and snaps playfully at his heels in an attempt to herd him away from the window.

"Hey!" Mick cries out with a laugh, snatching one foot after the other off the ground and away from Shadow's mouth. "You got somewhere you need to be?"

Shadow's bark is an unmistakable yes. He turns in my direction again, and with Mick now in tow, we chase the sea air until we are standing on the edge of a rippled reflection of every light Surfers Paradise has to offer.

The relatively calm night produces only the gentlest of waves. One after the other they roll toward the shore, where they spread thin bands of foam up onto the sand that catch the city lights and glow a fluorescent white. The water beyond the break shimmers with streaks of purple, white and green stretching away from us, until eventually fading into the black of the moonless horizon.

"How beautiful," Mick murmurs, once again stealing my thoughts. "I could stand here forever." He kicks his thongs off and wriggles the sand up into the gaps between his toes. "You ever been to the beach?" he asks Shadow.

Shadow answers with an eardrum-splitting puppy bark that not only says yes, but screams and guess what? It's my favourite thing *ever*! He then proves his love by diving head first onto his side, rolling onto his back, yipping and kicking his legs about until every inch of his body, outside of his eyeballs, is completely covered in sand.

When Shadow is satisfied that he can't fit one more grain of sand in anywhere, he jumps up, shakes himself clean, and begins tearing up and down the beach like a demented lunatic with way too much energy.

"Don't go too far!" I call as he flits past on one of his return runs.

He slides to a halt and looks up at me as if to groan, I know already, and waits impatiently for my ok before racing off again.

Mick, true to his 'I could stay here forever' comment, plonks himself onto his backside. He hesitantly eyes off the layer of sand now covering the bottom of his board shorts, then mumbles "Bugger it," and falls onto his back with his arms spread wide. He swipes his arms and legs from side to side to create a perfect sand angel, and then lies still, staring up into the night sky with pure contentment.

After checking to make sure there are no other night-time beachgoers at risk of being bowled over by Shadow – who's currently being teased into the shallows by a floating stick –

I lie down beside Mick and let my head fall back onto my hands.

"Can't see the stars," Mick says, and for a moment I allow myself to imagine he's talking to me.

"Too much glow from the city," I reply.

Mick indulges my imaginary conversation. "Wonder how many people have never been away from the city to see them. I loved the stars out west on the farm, lying out there with old Luna dog. They were so close, felt like you could almost reach up and grab one."

"I've only ever seen them like that once." I remember looking up on the night after we left Claire's.

Mick falls silent for a moment, and when he speaks again, his tone has taken a dive. "I wonder if she ever got to see them."

"Was she blind?" I ask, rolling on to my elbow to study his face. "How could you have had a blind working dog?"

He looks taunted by his memory, just as he did when he first spoke about his parents and the farm. The watery glistening in his eyes, that I remember brushing off as the shine from the truck stop floodlight, is back. Only this time it overflows into a single tear that slowly escapes the corner of his eye and trails toward his ear.

"I guess she's up *there* somewhere now," he says, leaving me to wonder whether or not Luna really was blind. "Maybe she's one of the stars." He doesn't bother to wipe the tear away.

I fall back onto the sand, realising this is the closest I've ever been to a boy and feeling a bit silly for my sudden shyness.

We lie in silence for a while, listening to the waves and watching Shadow splash in and out of the high tide line. The stick he was chasing drifts close enough to shore for him to wade out to, and hoping for a game, he plucks it from the water, drags it up the beach and drops it at my feet.

Mick doesn't seem to know how to take Shadow's stick placement. He follows Shadow's eyes, folds his eyebrows together and says something that could have come straight out of Rosie's mouth: "Why do I suddenly feel like we're not alone?"

21

You're kidding!

"Closer, Shadow. Bring the stick closer!" I can't believe I didn't think of this before! I might not be able to pick the stick up to throw it, but by getting Shadow to bring it closer, by making it obvious that his placement is anything but random, I can at least lead Mick to start questioning things.

Shadow does as asked. Without delay, he shoves his nose under the stick and nudges it closer to me.

The line between Mick's brows deepens.

"Now speak, Shadow. Speak!"

As quickly as if he already knew what I was about to say, Shadow barks. He then picks the stick up, impatiently drops it again, and lowers his profile in readiness to pounce.

Mick is now beyond curious. Keeping in line with the direction of Shadow's intense stare, he slowly lifts his hand and pokes a finger toward my shoulder. It closes in and for a breathless second, I wonder if either of us will feel anything. Mick looks every bit as hopeful as I am. But when his index finger reaches my arm and pokes into the curve below my shoulder, I feel nothing.

Utterly disappointed, I try to find some form of recognition in Mick's face, but his focus is fixed on his arm, where every single hair stands on end like he's stuck his finger in an electric socket. As quick as he can, he rips his hand away and flicks his eyes toward the ocean. It feels like he's not just dismissing the thought that he might not be alone, but outright rejecting it. "Idiot!" he scorns, his voice stained with self-disgust.

I want to reach out and make his hair stand on end again. I want to try and get through to him before he closes off completely, but Shadow has other plans.

With a dramatic and comically drawn out whimper, he shatters any hope I might have of connecting with Mick. He fills my mind with visions of him running down the beach after the stick and his begging is more annoying than that of a bored child: Helllooooo! I'm still waiting over here.

Mick can't help but lose himself in a fit of laughter. "Crikey, mate," he jeers. "I could almost write lyrics to that!" He picks the stick up, and without thinking to first check that the coast is clear, hurls it as far as he can toward the water's edge.

With Shadow hot on its trail, it's flight path takes a cringeworthy route directly toward a couple strolling through the sand, and before Mick can finish yelling "Look ou..." we see it smack into the side of one of the people and hear the resulting, highly unexpected, German-accented shriek.

"Ouahhh! What is this?"

Both Mick and I stiffen, trusting neither our ears nor eyes. "Oh, you're kidding me," Mick says.

"Is that...?" I ask, straining for a closer look.

"Ooooh! Hallo, Blue," the girl part of the couple coos, bending to welcome Shadow, who's come racing in for his stick.

"No way!" Mick clings to denial.

"Yep!" I lock it in. "It's Mila and Nico!"

***

Although still a hefty throw down the beach, I'm certain I can already see the twinkle in Mila's eyes as she homes in on Mick. She throws an arm overhead and calls out to him as though worried he might run away. Nico's behind her, waving over her shoulder like a long-lost friend and nudging her forward.

Without waiting for an invitation, the two push their way through the sand in our direction. Mila unapologetically slides in beside Mick, leaving little room for a toothpick between their shoulders, and swings her long, blonde lashes toward him in the same demure fashion as she did her hand earlier today.

"What a coincidence, *ja?*" she says, sounding less surprised and more like we finally found you!

Nico drops equally as close to Mick's other side, forcing me to shuffle out of the way so as not to be sat on, and leaving Mick no room for escape. He's put a shirt on since we last saw him. It's still got the shop's fold creases in it, and his choice of slogans on the front, '*wish you were beer*', perfectly aligns with my party-boy opinion of him.

He clamps one arm around Mick and shakes him playfully like an old buddy. "You are saving us today. Now we say…wait," he sticks his tongue between his teeth like he's about to bite it off, "ttthhhank you."

His self-pride alone is deserving of a reward; one he would have to take a breath between sentences to receive though. "You want to party? We go to a nightclub. Here is a great place to party. We buy drinks for you, *ja*?"

Mick's head bobs loosely from one side to the other, shaking up a smile that already has an excuse embedded into it. "I'd love to, but I can't. Sorry. I've gotta drive tomorrow, plus…" Right on cue, Shadow returns with his stick. "I've got this fella to look after."

"We take him too." Nico takes the stick and throws it. "We put a dress on him and say he is a midget."

Mila sneaks a disapproving glance behind Mick's back at Nico, "You can't say midget," she scoffs, using the opportunity to motion, with a head flick toward the city, for him to leave. "It's little person."

Nico picks up on his sister's request and obliges with two thumbs up. "Ok," he sings, a lot less secretive and clearly not caring to argue. "I go party." He wastes no time getting to his feet. "My sister can stay in your truck, *ja*, Mick?"

"Woah!" Mick is straight up behind Nico, leaving Mila in the sand with a fresh pout.

"Um, ah," he stutters, lost for a polite answer. "I don't really have the room," he finally manages. "Not with me and Mr. Shake."

Mila's confused. "His name is not Blue?"

"Ah," Mick's struggling to think straight. "Yeh, it was, but——"

Nico can't be bothered waiting for Mick to finish. "I am having an idea." He points a finger toward an imaginary light-bulb hovering above him. "Up the beach I am seeing a lot of people and rides, and lots of dogs too, and" he pulls the bottom corners of his new shirt out, "*beer*! Let's go and have some fun, *ja*?"

Neither Mick nor Mila look particularly enthralled by the idea, but Nico's words strike a chord with me. Mick possibly could use a break from being such a prematurely responsible adult. His boss said he was stuck here until tomorrow afternoon, which I believe, gives him plenty of time to 'enjoy yourself for once'. With that in mind, I take it upon myself to make the decision for him.

I call Shadow away from his stick. "Come on, let's check out these other dogs Nico's talking about."

Knowing Mick will follow, I lead Shadow toward the not-too-distant bright lights of the Gold Coast show.

"Where are you going?" Mick calls, chasing worriedly after Shadow as predicted,.

Nico laughs as he helps his sister to her feet. "You see? Even the dog wants to have some fun."

***

The walk along the beach reminds me of Shadow's and my first night on the road. Just as I did then, I allow the fear of uncertainty to creep in.

"We've been super lucky so far," I say, and Shadow tilts his head toward my voice. "What if we get to Sydney, leave Mick, and don't make it any further? What if we get all the way to Echuca and can't find Astrid? What if we run into someone who tries to hurt you and I can't stop them, or someone from the council catches you and takes you to the pound? What if, Shadow..." The idea that's been forming since this afternoon is one I'm sure Shadow will like. "What if we stay with Mick a little longer? He felt me before; I know he did. Or he felt something, at least. His mum knew I was there and I'm one hundred percent convinced he did too. I just can't figure out why he rejected it. I bet he wouldn't if Rosie told him the whole story. Even without that, I'm certain I could get through to him somehow, given enough time. But then, what if we do stay and he takes you back to Babinda? Then we have to escape him before he can find Claire and we have to start all over again from scratch. I wonder if there's a way we can stop him from trying to find her. I don't know what to do, Shadow."

The million little pictures that muddle my mind reach Shadow. He stops and locks his eyes onto mine, pushing the same image into my head as he did during my last moment of doubt: the one of he, Astrid and I standing on the side of a road. Only this time, instead of waiting euphorically for something, the something has arrived - and it's Mick.

Just like last time, I don't know whether the image is a vision or Shadow's wishful thinking.

"So you want to have them both, huh? Well, I guess we'll just see what tonight and tomorrow brings. See if we can get his attention again. If so, we might be able to figure out how to get him to take us the whole way. Maybe I could have you barking at Echuca street signs or something."

22

One can't hurt

Once inside the show-ground's gate, Nico's thirst for beer leads the rest of us on a weaving path, through the congestion of show enthusiasts, in search of a bar.

Mick seems reluctant to take in any of the atmosphere and keeps a firm eye on Shadow, nodding in polite acknowledgement every time Mila squeals, "Oooh! Look at this."

He forces a smile when Nico finally finds a bar set up inside a packed marquee, orders a round, and hands him a glass. "You have one beer, *ja*?"

"I really shouldn't. I've gotta drive tomorrow, remember?"

"*Ja*, but now is tonight," Nico pushes playfully. "And it is light beer, so one is ok." Nico addresses Shadow. "What do you say, puppy? Should he have one beer?"

Shadow looks at me for help figuring Nico's question out, and I have to ask myself what would I do? If Mick doesn't have to drive until tomorrow afternoon, which is still over twelve hours away, and it's only one light beer, then surely it can't hurt. It'll definitely be out of his system by then.

"Why not?" I shrug at Shadow. "I'd say it's ok. Say yes, Shadow, speak."

Shadow turns back to Nico and barks once.

"You see?" Nico elbows Mick hard enough to hurt. "Even your dog says you are no fun."

Mick smothers a laugh but allows his eyes to soften. He decides to play along. "How do you know that was a yes? Maybe it was a bark to say leave the poor bloke alone."

"Ok." Nico has an answer for everything. "We ask again! Mister Shake, bark once for *ja* and twice for *nein*. Should Mick have one drink?"

I quickly prompt Shadow.

"Fluke!" Mick jeers, his entire face spelling out the definition of disbelief.

Desperate to be included, Mila pipes up from the sidelines. "Ooh! I try. Mister Shake, should Mick go back to the beach and be alone and sad?"

"I wasn't sad." Mick's straight on the defensive.

"You looked sad. I have seen red in your eyes like a sad person."

Not wanting to give Mick the chance to fall back into melancholy, I quickly urge Shadow on. "Speak again, Shadow. Speak."

Shadow, loving the whole centre of attention thing, complies with two full-throated barks that each cause his front paws to lift off the ground.

"You see?" Nico's arms fly out like a magician, revealing empty hands.

"So you think I'm boring, huh?" Mick teases Shadow.

Someone behind us shouts, "Shut that bloody dog up."

Mila snatches her glass off the counter and grabs hold of Mick. "Come," she frets. "We should go before they are telling us to get out."

As Mila drags Mick away, Nico calls over his shoulder, "I bring drinks. I just order one more *und* then I come out."

Shadow and I hastily follow Mick and Mila out of the marquee. We pick our way through the thick of the crowd and out into the open, toward a demountable grandstand set up under the stars.

Nico eventually joins us with his and Mick's drinks, and thoughtfully enough, Hot dogs for everyone, including Shadow. He instantly empties his glass, immediately starts to fidget, and decides to run back to the marquee for a second round.

When he returns, he's brought back four more glasses, half of which he pours down his own throat, before passing the remaining two over to Mick and Mila.

Bowing to the peer pressure from not only the two Germans, but Shadow also, Mick sips away his first beer. By the end of it, he loosens up so much that he allows Nico to hand him a second without argument.

"Two should be fine," I say to Shadow, watching Mick take a fresh sip and then sit the glass down. "I can't imagine he'll have any more. That's if he even finishes it. He's not an idiot."

In front of us, a small grassy ring surrounded by blinding floodlights has been cordoned off by a string of gently flapping orange flags. There's a makeshift judges table set up at one end and a flock of costumed competitors at the other, each accompanied by a single, exceptionally eager-looking dog.

Whatever the competition is, it must be about to start, because there's a steward running around with a clipboard full of names and calling out for the first competitor.

A lady in a red-tasselled jumpsuit steps forward with a black and white border collie. Both appear confident enough to have done this before as they are ushered into the ring.

I glance back at Mick, who seems oddly comfortable squished again like the middle pea in a pod between Mila and Nico, despite the miles of room either side. He's chewing on his Hot dog like it's the last meal he'll ever have and elbowing Mila in the ribs to listen to his joke.

"I knew this bloke," he starts through a full mouth, "who was so competitive that, on his death bed, as he took his last breath, he said, 'Staring competition. Go!'"

"Oh!" Mila frowns. "That is so sad." She grabs Mick's hand and gives it a gentle squeeze.

To my surprise, rather than awkwardly pull away, Mick squeezes back and comfortingly explains, "It's just a joke: don't worry."

At the end of the ring where the table has been set up, three rather pretentious-looking judges take their seats. Shortly after, the middle one catches our attention with a test tap against a megaphone. She straightens her navy blue pantsuit that's ironed enough to stand on its own, eyes the minimal turnout with bitter disappointment, and addresses her audience with a tone that could freeze the wings off a passing butterfly.

"This is the National Dog Dancing Association's first competition for the year."

"Yes, sir." Mick salutes loudly, shocking the judge into a begrudging pause, and Mila and I into a stunned giggle.

The judge follows Mick's voice all the way back to his face, the details of which she, without question, imprints on her brain as she continues. "Tonight's winners will be selected from two categories: Judges' Choice and People's Choice. We'll begin with the Judges' Choice now."

Someone has taken *now* literally, as seconds later a doof-doof explodes from a pair of speakers mounted high up on a light pole behind the ring.

The lady in the red suit beckons her collie to her side with a finger-click. The pair stand facing the judges in the ring's centre and the lady seems to be attempting to explain, through a series of winding hand movements, that the music started before she and her dog were ready.

"Stop the music!" the principal judge barks. "I haven't introduced our first competitors yet."

The music comes to an abrupt halt. The lady salutes the judges with a petite bow and strikes a straight-legged pose, reaching both hands up into the air.

"Our first competitors," the judge squints to read the names from her list, "are Amanda Benz and Detroit."

A scattered round of half-hearted applause follows, and as the music bursts for a second time through the speakers, I am immediately awestruck by the black and white Collie, Detroit.

"Look, Shadow. Look!" I nudge him away from his greasy

dinner. Shadow places one paw over his half-eaten Hot dog, just in case one of the other dogs should come sniffing, and watches as Detroit mimics his red-suited owner.

The Collie stands tall on his hind legs and raises both front paws as high as possible over his head. His owner, keeping time with the beat, bends her knees in a squat and then straightens up again. Detroit, lowering himself onto his haunches and lifting himself up again, follows her movements exactly.

Together the two perform a well-rehearsed routine unlike anything I could have imagined: simultaneous figure-eights, belly rolls, jumps, twists, back-ups; and each time the chorus of the extremely fitting song 'Put Your Hands Up For Detroit' comes around, the pair pirouette side by side with arms and paws stretched proudly into the air.

The routine's end incites a hefty applause from both the formerly half-hearted crowd and a hoard of new onlookers who hurriedly gather to catch the next act.

I check to see how Mick's enjoying things and almost get a shock. His contentment has rapidly escalated to feverish excitement. He's ripped his hand out of Mila's, and together with Nico, is clapping and cheering as robustly as even the loudest of the spectators.

A duo, who obviously couldn't be bothered with costumes, performs next. They are almost instantly eliminated when the black German shepherd succumbs to his natural instincts and marks his territory on the leg of the judges' table. Unfortunately his aim is a little off, resulting in the cotton-panted leg of the judge on the left requiring paper towels and a bottle of water – pronto.

Mick inappropriately cheers the German shepherd on, and then, as if unable to sit still, finds a golden retriever wearing a bumblebee costume to point and hysterically laugh at.

I can't decide if I should be worried about his behaviour or just enjoy it. Does he get like this every time he has *one* drink?

Shadow, as expected, is also having a fantastic time. Each time Mick unrestrainedly applauds the end of another act, Shadow jumps to his feet and barks with equal vigour. He's clearly revelling in the fact that due to the surrounding volume, I haven't had a need to tell him to shoosh.

Mick and Nico ecstatically cheer the competition to its end. They wolf-whistle as Detroit and his red-suited companion are announced the winners, and clap to the beat of the people's choice category's first song. The song plays into its opening verse without any sign of an accompanying competitor, leaving the entire gathering of spectators scratching their heads.

The middle judge grapples across the table for her competitors' list. In doing so, she knocks over a mug of coffee sitting dangerously close and saturates the piece of paper, reducing it to an indecipherable slop. Her words can't be heard over the music, but she seems to be questioning her fellow judges about copies. Both shrug their shoulders and raise empty hands. She looks ready to boil over, and as she opens her mouth to yell at them over the music, someone takes the opportunity to press stop, causing her fury to be heard all the way across the ring. "Well! Where are they?"

A snicker ripples through the crowd before they hush themselves to silence.

Seizing an idea, Nico jumps to his feet. He criss-crosses his arms overhead and hollers, "Here they are."

The entire audience, along with all three judges, turn to the sound of Nico's voice and follow the point of his finger across to Mick and Shadow.

Glaring down her Doberman nose, the middle judge snorts at the idea. She protests alone though. The crowd makes that clear with a slow-building clap that soon resonates around the ring.

Caught unawares by the sudden attention, Mick can't quite decide on how to greet his new audience. His face skips from 'what?' to 'nooo,' bounces through 'you think?' and eventually lands on a surprisingly certain 'yeh, I could do that!' He then switches his starry eyes over to Shadow. "You reckon we should?"

Shadow, as usual, is itching to move. Caught up in the music, the cheering, and now the prompting of Mick's question, he fearlessly lifts himself up onto his hind legs and raises both front paws, just as he saw Detroit do earlier. He follows through with a solo bark which Nico accepts as reason enough to throw his arms out and shout, "*Jaaaa*! Welcome everybody, Mick and Mister Shake."

23

Let's dance

With Shadow prancing as proud as a high-stepping pony by his side, Mick bounds off the grandstand. He then remembers his almost untouched second beer, gallops back, sculls it for motivation, and makes his way to the dog-dancing ring, bowing and fist-pumping the air like an actor in some B-grade comedy show.

Half the crowd cheer his over-zealous display on, while the other half succumb to rolling their eyes.

The three judges are all seated again, the outer two amused enough to out-vote their scowling colleague in the middle. "To be fair," one says, trying not to laugh at Mick, who's now in the centre of the ring performing some sort of helicopter warm-up movement with Shadow circling him like a rogue cow, "we didn't actually take registrations for the people's choice."

"Anyone can enter," the other adds sheepishly.

The middle judge, clearly divided between putting an end to the lunacy now and allowing the idiot in the ring to bring about his own demise, takes once again to her megaphone and directs a prickly warning at Mick. "This is a *serious* competition!"

Whoever it is that's in charge of the music clearly has a knack for choosing the most inconvenient moments to press stop and play, because before the judge can say another word, a new explosion of doof - doof music drowns her out and immediately forces her, along with her distaste, back to the confines of her chair.

About five beats in, after running out of warm-up moves, Mick realises he has no idea what to do. He drops a hip and begins with a subtle, rhythmic knee-bend. He seems to be trying to buy himself some time while searching his audience for ideas.

I can't believe how quickly the alcohol has affected him. I guess that's why he wasn't so keen on having any. He must know he gets like this.

The clap of the crowd peters out quicker than expected. They're already getting bored and I think I just heard a boo from somewhere in the back.

Shadow's finally realised Mick's not a cow, and since neither Mick nor I have given him anything specific to do, he's using his pent-up energy to deepen a small hole he's found in the grass.

I wonder what will happen if Mick and Shadow do get booed out, and if Mick has to return to the grandstand with his own pent-up energy. Is he one of those people who continue to drink themselves into a stupor? If he does, will the alcohol bring up his memories of losing the family farm and send him into depression? Or worse, is he the kind to turn violent? I really don't think I want to find those things out. Shadow's grown so fond of Mick, and I have too. I'd rather not give him the chance to continue drinking. In which case, I figure I'll have to keep him occupied, and what better place to do it than in the centre of a dog-dancing ring with a dog who can perfectly understand my every command.

***

Shadow's nose is out of his new hole the second I call his name. "Shadow, remember that time you tried to jump the fence, but didn't quite get to the top and ended up doing a backflip? Well, Mick is the fence. Go!"

With the image from a couple of years ago fresh in his mind, Shadow scampers to Mick's left. He takes a few steps back, lines Mick's height up, and launches himself from a standstill into the air. Reaching Mick's shoulder height, he brings his full body to a vertical, and with all four paws outstretched, collides into Mick's side. From there, he pushes himself backward, flips expertly through the air and returns, sure-footed, to the ground.

It would have been a flawless display if the force of Shadow's push didn't send Mick into an out-of-control, sideways stumble. But it did, and Mick's right foot has just found Shadow's newly dug hole. I think I feel the jarring of his knee more than he does; he's too busy trying not to fall over.

The thong, attached to that same foot, twists underneath. Mick lunges forward, trips up as his feet wind themselves into a tangle, and instinctively throws both arms out in front to brace for the inevitable fall.

He looks like an Egyptian mummy as he plummets toward

the ground. There's absolutely no grace in the way he cries out, "Wooooaahhh!" but his landing is super-impressive.

Rather than fall flat on his face, he hits the ground with outstretched arms and enough momentum behind him to send his legs and lower body swinging high up over his head.

The manoeuvre dislodges his twisted thong. With hundreds of pairs of eyes trailing it like a rocket to the moon, it flies through the air and lands with a victorious slap against none other than the middle judge's head.

The judge, angered further by the ensuing uproar of laughter, screams out of her seat, popping all the blood vessels in her cheeks at the same time. Her eyes flare with enough heat to start a bushfire as she tries to call an end to the madness, but Mr. Music turns the volume up another notch, prompting the sheepish colleague on her left to feign sympathy and cautiously pull her back down to silence.

All eyes are back on Mick. He teeters in the handstand position for a gloriously long time until gravity eventually takes over and pulls him backward. Trying his hardest to correct his balance, he bends his back and flails his legs as wildly as if he were running on air. The closer his feet come to landing, the more speed they gather, and by the time they hit the ground behind his head, they do so with enough propulsion to lurch him once again into a perfectly straight, upright stand.

"Mummy!" I hear a little kid squeal. "The man and the dog did backflips together. Why doesn't *our* dog do backflips with *me*?"

The mum's answer is so matter-of-fact, it impresses even me. "These people train their dogs for *years*, honey."

Shaking off sudden dizziness, Mick holds his bare foot up. He must be wondering what happened to his thong. He looks at the grass behind him like he's trying to comprehend what just happened, and when he realises he's just done a backflip, he throws his hands up high above the imbecilic, self-satisfied grin that's taken over his face and shouts, "Ta-da!"

The crowd seems divided between awe and distaste.

"You reckon he meant to do that?" I hear someone ask their neighbour. "Doesn't look too well-rehearsed if you ask me. That bloke looks drunk, and that dog doesn't look even close to smart enough to be *that* well trained. Look at it. It's sitting there licking itself!"

While the comment evokes a parental defensiveness in me, I have to concede it is warranted. Unlike most of the other dogs, who tentatively watch their master's every move, Shadow's forgotten all about Mick. Instead his nose is buried deep in an itchy investigation happening embarrassingly close to the lower base of his tail.

Mick seems to be having a moment of uncertainty. His eyes slightly glaze over and he wobbles a little on his feet. For a second, I wonder if I should be concerned. Almost instantly, he dismisses my fear by blinking himself into focus again and beaming to the crowd as though it's all part of a well-rehearsed plan.

Unfortunately nobody's buying it.

The only way I can think of to help him out is to get Shadow to also pretend to be drunk. Quickly calling him away from his itch, I show him how to stumble a full circle around Mick, then how to fall over as though he can't hold himself up, and then how to play dead. He does it like a true actor, and unlike Mick's display, the crowd loves it.

More astounded by Shadow's performance than any of the onlookers, Mick decides to see what else Shadow is capable of. As if he's talking to another human, he calls him out with a head banging move and then shouts, "I bet you can't do that."

"I bet you can," I dare Shadow and show him exactly how.

Mick laughs so hard he convulses.

Shadow's head thrashes up and down wildly enough to do permanent spinal damage.

"That's enough," I shriek, but my voice gets lost in the cheering.

Mick throws himself straight into a new move, calling Shadow out for a new dare. It's the running man this time – how am I supposed to explain *that*?

Shadow's running man isn't quite as good as the version I try to show him. Without arms to pump back and forth, he looks more like he's just jogging on the spot. But he's so energetic about it, it's impressive nonetheless.

Deciding he won't be outdone, Mick begins testing every dance move he can think of and marvelling at Shadow each time he follows suit. From really bad ballet moves, to awkwardly inappropriate hip thrusting, nothing gets left out. He even attempts the moonwalk. On his own, he would most definitely have been booed out of the ring by now, but with Shadow beside him, mimicking his every move as good as his four legs will allow, the act is a hit.

As the song nears its end, Shadow becomes too wound up to continue following my direction and decides to cut loose with a stunt of his own. He sizes Mick up, gives himself a good run-up, and then scales Mick's back like a wall. This time, instead of doing another backflip to the ground, he clambers onto Mick's shoulders and somehow manages to stay there.

With one front and one back paw fighting for space either side of Mick's neck, he tests his balance by first lifting one hind leg. He doesn't fall and so follows with the other. I hear a collective sharp inhalation from the crowd and the deafening silence that follows as everyone, myself included, holds their breath.

Before my mothering instincts can get the better of me and have me ordering Shadow down to safety, he does it: a brilliantly straight, perfectly balanced, front paw stand on Mick's shoulders.

I don't know whether to laugh or cry. I can barely hear myself think over the flabbergasted uproar of the crowd. He must have been watching the other dogs closer than I thought.

Gaining superhero confidence now, Shadow carefully lowers his back paws again and puts everyone in stitches by drooping his body limply over Mick's head like a hat.

"Cover his eyes with your paws," I shriek, showing him how while completely swollen with pride.

Shadow complies, and a second later Mick cries out with convincing sincerity, "I can't see."

He reaches up, fumbles Shadow's paws aside, looks up and whimsically asks, "Hey! How did you get up there?"

Lost in his own goofiness, Mick holds Shadow's paws and has every child in the crowd squealing with delight when he says, "Peek-a-boo!"

The game lasts only a couple of rounds before Shadow begins to slide dangerously to one side. Anticipating the unfolding tragedy, I quickly shout out "Down, Shadow!"

Managing to right himself long enough to push off, he executes another impressive backflip to the ground.

By the time the song ends, there is not a dry eye to be seen. To top the performance off, right on cue with the last beat, Mick feigns exhaustion and lets himself fall to the ground. He's very convincing, lying on his back with arms spread wide and gasping for air like a fish. The sight of him brings an idea to mind and so I line Shadow up for his final act – pretend CPR.

I direct Shadow to place one paw above Mick's chest, and then to tap it up and down. Afterwards I show him how to give mouth-to-mouth and he repeats the action as perfectly as his snout will allow. I can fully appreciate the laughing cries of "yuk" and "gross" that accompany Shadow's tongue repeatedly finding its way into Mick's mouth, and the wild cheering as Mick brushes Shadow off so he can breathe properly.

Shadow returns to tapping Mick's chest, and Mick allows his arms to flop back to the ground. He lies there, a little paler than usual, and sucking in deep breaths of air while Shadow taps away.

"Nobody can top that," somebody hollers, sending the crowd wilder.

"That's bloody gold," another onlooker shouts. "You win

hands down. I've never seen anything like it. Sure that's not a little person in a dog costume?"

The cheering lasts long enough for Shadow to get bored and return to the itch under his tail. As he leans away, I see Mick reach out and attempt to grab hold of him, like he's trying to get his attention. He should have his breath back, at least somewhat by now, but he's still gasping. When his hand finally does make contact with Shadow's tail, he clutches onto it and tugs hard enough to incite a surprised yelp.

Shadow spins around to see what the tail tugging is about. I expect Mick to give him a pat of apology and then pick himself up off the ground, but he doesn't move. Something's not right.

His struggle for breath seems more laboured than it should be, and if I'm not mistaken, it looks like there's a whisper of fear creeping into his hazel eyes. I don't think it's part of the act anymore, but I don't know what else it can be. All I know for certain is, "Shadow! Something's wrong with Mick."

24

Checked shirt

My change of attitude pulls the plug on Shadow's playfulness and all the fun drains out of him like water gurgling down the sink. He sucks his panting tongue back into his mouth and clenches it shut. His tail falls between his legs, his ears lay themselves flat, and his eyes turn toward me like two giant question marks. What's wrong with him, he wants to know. What do I do?

On one side of the ring, a woman steps hesitantly forward from her cheering peers. She halts mid-clap and studies Mick with apprehension. "Is he alright?" I hear her ask. Her question aimed at no one in particular. "I think..." She pauses, undecided.

A couple of other onlookers follow her cue into silence. I search the grandstand for Nico and Mila, half-expecting to see them worriedly racing in to help Mick. When I do find them, while Mila looks equally as surprised by the turn of events as the rest of the crowd, Nico's face has a curious air of guilt about it.

Mila tears her eyes from Mick to ask her brother, "Should we do something?"

She immediately notices the guilt and I hear the accusation in her voice as she glowers at him. "What have you done?"

I know that whatever Nico's answer is, it will be something I can't afford to miss. I'm beside Nico before he can even open his mouth, but everything, from his eyes that won't settle on any specific direction, to the zipped-shut line of his tucked-in lips, contradicts the innocent words that come out of his mouth. "I have just given him beer."

Mila see's the lie and forces more information out of him with a furious slap across the arm. "Nico?"

"Ok, ok!" Nico seems determined to downplay the situation. "I have just put a little bit of the stuff that we bought in Townsville in his beer. You remember? We have taken some on that night when we party on the beach. I didn't think it would hurt. I just wanted him to have some fun."

Mila's jaw couldn't drop further if it were weighed down by a brick and thrown in the ocean to drown. "How much have you given him?"

"Just a little bit in his first beer: just to make him relax."

Untrusting of her brother, Mila squints to study Mick. His hand that was wrapped around Shadow's tail, lies once again by his side. Along with his other hand, it balls itself into a fist so tight that his fingernails cut into his palm.

Mila has every right to suspect Nico's not telling the whole truth. "And..." She probes further.

Nico can no longer look past Mick's dire state. The sight of him twitching, and silently gasping for help, chases away any hopes Nico might have had of convincing himself that everything will be fine. There's no more grin, no more false innocence. Just the face of a frightened little boy when he pulls a small vial from his shorts pocket with trembling hands and cringingly shows it to Mila.

"I gave him the whole lot."

***

Mick is sweating so profusely that his entire face is dripping and his clothes are wringing wet. After hearing Nico's confession, I couldn't stay away any longer. He's not drunk, his drink was spiked, and all the drug education lectures from school are now screaming at me to get him help fast.

The woman who first stepped forward notices, at the same time as I do, how Mick's entire body begins to spasm, cramping and then uncramping, over and over again. "Somebody do something!" she shrieks, her voice echoing over the now ghastly silent crowd.

Shadow's beside himself with helplessness. He's circling Mick, yelping, nudging, snapping and crying for him to get up, but Mick doesn't hear him. He's too consumed by the poison that's coursing through his bloodstream.

I hear someone behind me. "Excuse me, move, get out of the way," and a second later, two paramedics drop to their knees beside Mick.

"What are you thinking?" one asks.

"Possible overdose," the other answers. "Check his vitals, quick." He raises his voice, "Can someone hold the dog, please."

My ears begin to drum, as if someone's started the music again; this time choosing an out-of-control techno-beat. A quick glance at Shadow, who's trying to fight his way out of the grasp of the lady who called for help, and another glance at the crowd, proves no one else can hear it. It's getting quicker, louder, falling in and out of rhythm, and when I look at Mick, I notice it perfectly matches the rapid rise and fall of his chest. The sound, coupled with the sight, drowns everything else out until it becomes almost hypnotic. It draws me like a pied piper's rat down to Mick's side where, even though I don't believe for a second there's anything I can do to help, it overwhelms me with a single, pointless urge. I need to feel Mick's heart.

I reach my hand over his chest, and as I lower my palm, it begins to tingle and heat up. It's the same feeling as when I first broke out of the nothing with Shadow, and just as it did then, it gets warmer and warmer until it feels like it could burn at any moment.

"Mick!" I plead, searching his eyes for any sign of awareness.

Afraid of, and at the same time welcoming the burn, I press my hand down further, and as it touches Mick's chest, I feel not only the sting of the fire that seems to scorch his insides, but something else underneath. Something I shouldn't be able to touch. I feel the soft flannelette fabric of Mick's shirt.

Mick's chest suddenly convulses. It heaves into the air, causing his back to arch off the ground and his eyes to pop into focus.

One of the paramedics instantly begins clicking his fingers in front of Mick's face. "You there? You there, mate? Look here. Look at me."

Mick doesn't follow the man's fingers. His eyes are too focused on something else that seems to shock, terrify, and captivate him all at the same time. His eyes are focused—on *me.*

"Get him on the stretcher," I hear, and as Mick is rolled onto his side, my hand is torn away from his chest: along with it, the fiery heat, his focus, the drum of techno music, and the beating of his heart.

Shadow finally wriggles free of his captor. He bulldozes his way past the paramedics to Mick's side-turned face, and consumed by desperation, hopelessly re-attempts the mouth-to-mouth move that only moments ago had the crowd in stitches.

I hear a child start to cry, then someone say, "Oh god! The poor baby; I can't watch."

One more scout through the audience shows a grave wall of faces, but there's two less than there were before, and it comes as little surprise to realise that Nico and Mila are gone.

Mick is lifted onto the stretcher and rolled into the back of a waiting ambulance.

The cry-for-help lady, who also tried to hold Shadow back, offers to follow with him to the hospital, and before I can wrap my head around the gravity of our situation, Shadow and I are being flung around the back seat of a stranger's car as it zips through the Gold Coast streets behind the ambulance.

***

The ambulance punches through the traffic with lights flashing and sirens wailing. It cautions its way through intersections where our driver is forced to stop and wait, and eventually speeds too far ahead for us to be able to keep our eyes on it.

"It's alright," our driver says, as Shadow anxiously climbs forward onto the front seat, trying to spot the ambulance again. "I know the way. I'll get you there, pup."

It isn't long before we are turning off the street to follow a huge, red sign plastered with the word Emergency. We pull up behind one of two ambulances - both of which seem to have only just arrived - and before our driver has the time to let Shadow out, the back doors of the ambulance directly in front swing open.

Two paramedics, in no particular rush, roll out a stretcher. As they slowly wheel it toward the emergency ward's automatic doors, we catch sight of the sheet-covered body on top.

A gravely solemn "Oh no," is the most our driver can manage.

Shadow starts to whimper.

"It might not be him," I say. "He might be in the other ambulance." I try everything I can to sound hopeful, despite the dread building in the pit of my stomach, but I know myself it's not true. I know it even before the breeze picks up and lifts the sheet a little on one side, and when Shadow sees the lifeless arm lying underneath, he knows it too.

It's covered in a flannelette fabric checkered shirt - just like Mick's.

25

Olivia

"Hi, honey."

"What's wrong? You sound miserable."

"Yeah. I...um. God...I saw somebody die tonight."

"What? Who? What happened? Are you ok?"

"Yeh...I'm fine. I've got a dog with me from the show. I was watching the dog dancing during my break at the food stand. One of the competitors collapsed and they rushed him to hospital. I followed with his dog. We just saw him come out of the ambulance...all covered up. Oh god, it was horrible. Only a really young guy too, maybe twenty or so. I've still got the dog. I didn't know what else to do with him. I've left my name with the hospital so the guy's family can collect the dog, but I thought I might bring him home tonight. The poor thing is so distraught, I just couldn't leave him. Is Olivia still up?"

"Oh, honey, that's awful. You poor thing. Yeh, she's still up, being a typical five-year-old and refusing to go to sleep till Mum gets home. Bring the dog here; we'll look after him."

***

The shock sinks deeper, the further we get from the hospital. Our driver silently steers her car as though on autopilot, the muscles above her cheeks twitching like she might burst into tears at any moment.

Shadow's returned to the back seat with me. His eyes are glued to the street behind, even though the hospital is well out of view.

I know he refuses to believe what he's seen. I know he's hoping that, by some miracle, Mick will all of a sudden appear behind us, running after the car, shouting, 'Wait! I'm alive.' But there's no Mick. There never will be, and for the moment, I'm far too numb to explain this to Shadow.

It might be five minutes later that we pull up outside a small, suburban brick home; it might be an hour. I didn't pay any attention to the direction in which we travelled. We could be back in Cairns by now; I wouldn't know. All I can think about is, once again, how on earth do we get to Astrid's from here.

Outside lights click on and a man rushes worriedly to greet our driver. He opens her door, helps her from the car, and as he embraces her, she finally unloads the shock of the evening's events onto his shoulder.

"Just give me a minute," she says, eventually pulling herself together. "I don't want Olivia to see me like this."

She opens the car up for Shadow and I, and with no idea what else to do, we quietly get out, and follow her into the house.

As the front door shuts behind us, a little girl in unicorn pyjamas, with a plump, freckled face trailed by wild ginger curls, frolics into the room. "Mummy's home!" she screeches.

She catches sight of Shadow and her eyes light up as though it's Christmas morning. "You brought me a dog?"

The man gently grabs her by the wrist before she can run over to Shadow. "Shhh! He's not ours, honey. He just needs our help for a little while. He's very sad at the moment, so we have to be a little bit quiet, ok?"

The girl listens to her dad and tones herself down to a whisper. "Why is he sad?"

"Because he's lost his daddy and he's all alone at the moment. So we have to be especially nice to him, ok, honey?"

"Where did his daddy go?"

Both parents look at each other before the mum decides to proceed. "His daddy's gone to heaven, sweetheart," She says softly. "Just like Poppy did last year."

Seeing Shadow slumped, his head between his shoulder blades and his eyes turned to the floor, the little girl wipes a sprouting tear away before it can roll down her cheek. "Poor puppy," she says. She then lightens a little, turns her doll-like eyes in my direction, and says, "At least he's still got his mummy."

***

The little girl's words echo in my head long after her parents dismiss them, send her off to bed, and tuck themselves in for the night.

Unsure of how safe it was to leave a strange cattle dog roaming through their house, they'd decided to shut Shadow in a spare room. Kindly enough, they made it one with a soft single bed, a nightstand lamp left on, and a bowl of water on a towel in one carpeted corner.

I lie on my side, on top of a peach-coloured doona with

my head on a matching pillow and my arm curled around Shadow.

"She saw me," I repeat for the umpteenth time, still unwilling to believe it myself. "How is that possible?"

A barely audible squeak catches our attention, and as Shadow lifts his head from his half of the pillow, the door cracks ajar and little Olivia peers timidly into the room.

Keeping one hand wrapped around the doorknob, she uses the other to nervously twirl her hair while she gazes first at Shadow, and then, leaving no more room for doubt, undeniably at me.

I have no idea what to do other than stare back. Will I frighten her if I move? Can I say hello without her running screaming from the room? Does she understand what I am?

Shadow breaks the ice with a brief tail wag. It's doused more in self-pity than welcome, but it relaxes Olivia enough for her to remove her hand from the doorknob and take a step closer.

In the shyest of voices, she asks, "Can I please pat your dog?"

I don't know if it's her innocence, or the fact that she's actually speaking to me. It might be Mick's death, or an accumulation of everything that's happened since my accident, but the most I can manage is a stunned nod. After that, without warning, I feel the tears come. Thick and fast, they spill out of my eyes, stream over my cheeks and drip off my chin. After the events of today, the mere sight of this spindly little girl tiptoeing across the room in her unicorn pyjamas makes me realise there's always a little bit of light to be found in even the darkest of days. She can see me!

"Why are you sad?" Olivia asks, climbing like a monkey on to the bed at my feet.

I don't have a hope of turning off the waterworks or the smile that bores through it. "They're happy tears," I choke. "I'm not sad; I'm happy."

She absentmindedly begins to stroke Shadow's back. He sits up to investigate this new person, and as he sniffs curiously around her face, she lets out a giggle. As quick as anything, she claps a hand over her mouth and shoots a fearful glance at the door. "Don't tell Mummy and Daddy I'm here," she whispers. "I'm supposed to be in bed and Mummy might start crying again."

"Why would she cry?" I ask, full of curiosity and finally managing to curb my own tears.

"Mummy cried when I told her Poppy visited me from heaven. Are you from heaven too?"

The question seems completely normal for her. Shadow's finished sniffing and is lying back down again, and she continues to stroke his back as though my answer is neither here nor there.

"Um." I have to admit I don't know the answer exactly. "No, I don't think I am."

"Were you naughty? Daddy said naughty people don't go to heaven."

"Where did he say they go?"

Olivia shrugs. "But you know what I think?" She sounds excited to tell me.

"What?"

"I think all the naughty people don't go anywhere. I think

they stay with the people they hurt until they don't hurt any-more. Is that why you're not in heaven?"

I begin to shake my head and then realise Olivia's words couldn't ring truer. I *was* naughty. I caused my own death. I hurt so many people - especially Shadow. And until now, I haven't even stopped to think about the truck driver who couldn't avoid hitting me. What about him or her? Are they ok? Did they also die? Have I also hurt *their* families?

The tears return, harder this time, as the realisation sets in. "Yes, Olivia," I have to concede. "I was naughty. And I think you're right. I think maybe I do have to stay until the ones I hurt don't hurt anymore."

Olivia shows no judgment, only curiosity, as she asks, "What did you do?"

I don't immediately know how to explain texting and dri-ving, or a car crash, to a five-year-old. I don't want to frighten her with gory details or confuse her with explanations. I think of all the safe driving ads on TV that I always switched off. I think of Shadow's warnings that I ignored and all the common sense I failed to use. "I didn't listen, Olivia. That's what I did wrong. I didn't listen."

Olivia holds quiet for a moment, as if processing my an-swer. I expect her to want to know more, but she seems happy enough to change the subject. "What's your dog's name?"

"This is Shadow."

"He's soft. Why are you here?"

"We're, um...we're on our way somewhere."

"Where?"

"Do you know where Echuca is?"

Olivia blanks out.

"I think it's somewhere near Melbourne," I continue. "Do you know where Melbourne is?"

This time I couldn't have asked a more stupid question.

"Of course I do." Olivia's little tongue clicks. "That's where my mummy used to live before I was born. All my cousins live there too. Mummy and I caught a bus there at Christmas time. We had to get up really early to walk to the big shops down the road. That's where the bus stop is. Are you going to catch the bus there too?"

The idea doesn't sound too bad. Provided I can somehow sneak Shadow on, a bus could take us the entire way in a matter of days. "So you had to get up really early to catch it, huh?" I ask.

"Yep. It was dark."

"I don't suppose you know what day it was?"

Olivia responds without thinking: "Sunday."

"Are you sure?"

"Yep. Mummy swore because she had to get up early. Can I tell you what she said?"

"Are you allowed to swear?"

Nothing about Olivia says yes.

"Well, if it's not too bad, I promise I won't tell if you don't."

"Ok," she says, glancing again toward the door. She cups one hand around the side of her mouth and leans in close. "She said, 'who drives a bus this early on a *bloody* Sunday?'"

Springing back to her end of the bed, she sucks her lips in to hide her cheeky smile and watches the door for a moment. When no one comes through it to reprimand her, she shoots me a wide-eyed "Phew!" and goes back to stroking Shadow.

"Olivia, can you tell me how to get to the big shops?"

Sliding off the bed, Olivia waves me over to follow her to the room's one window. She pulls the bottom of the curtain aside enough to point out over a row of dark houses and toward a towering, bright white sign only a block or two away. "They're there."

"And tomorrow's Sunday," I realise out loud. "One more thing, Olivia. Do you think you could open the front door for us, please?"

26

Sydney

After making Olivia promise to lock the door behind us, and waiting to hear the tell-tale click, Shadow and I start in the direction of the shopping centre, or big shops, as Olivia so sweetly called it.

I can't be sure of how late in the night, or early in the morning, it is. So much has happened since it got dark. It feels like this one night has already lasted forever and may never end.

Shadow's too tired to rush. Worn out from running on the beach, dancing, only eating a Hot dog, and then the thought of Mick, he's lost any initiative to keep moving.

I feel it all too. I understand it perfectly, but this bus might be our only chance to get to Astrid. So, with a heart just as heavy as his, I ask him to please push through it.

The neighbouring houses are mostly dark, and except for a lone taxi that rushes by, the streets are empty. As we get closer to the shopping centre, we see a row of well-lit bus shelters lined up outside a supermarket entrance. On the bench seat of one of them, there's a man slumped, lightly snoring, against the shelter wall with a suitcase at his feet.

"That might be it, Shadow." I allow the two of us to finally slow our pace.

Not wanting to be seen, I lead Shadow behind the shelter, where he tiredly drops to the concrete and closes his eyes. The man on the seat in front doesn't stir, and within minutes, Shadow's battling him to a snore-off.

I don't know how much time passes while we wait. Every now and then a taxi drives by, slows down in hopes of a lucky fare, then moves on again. Eventually the shadows begin to lose their depth. The outlines of the trees surrounding the shopping centre's car park become visible against the sky, and as the easily recognisable song of a magpie welcomes the dawn, a bus signed 'Melbourne via Sydney' turns off the street toward us.

Both Shadow and the man in the shelter wake to the sound of the bus's brakes. The driver steps out and unlocks the undercarriage to help the man load his suitcase.

"Quiet." I whisper, leading Shadow out from behind and to the far side of the shelter. Keeping a close eye on the driver, I wait for his head to disappear inside the undercarriage as he pushes the bag in to a secure spot.

"Come on, Shadow. Quick."

As quiet as a mouse, Shadow follows me up the steps. Half a dozen passengers are already seated inside. Some are sound asleep, others are preoccupied with their devices, and a couple are busy watching the two men outside. I signal for Shadow to stay low and tread quietly. We make it to the third row of seats, almost past the couple looking out the window, when one of the passengers in front drops a water bottle which rolls down the aisle and comes to a stop at Shadow's feet.

The passenger leans into the aisle to retrieve their bottle and I hear a slightly startled, "Oh! There's a dog in here."

Another passenger on the opposite side hears it as well and feels the need to confirm the sighting loud enough to bring more heads leaning into the aisle to gawk at Shadow.

"What do you think it's doing?" one asks.

"Shouldn't be on here," another says. "Better tell the driver."

Five seconds later, the entire bus is awake.

A little boy, somewhere down the back, starts crying. His mother bangs on the window and calls out to the driver, "There's a dog on here. My kid's scared of dogs. Get it off!"

The driver hurries away from the baggage compartment, leaving it open for the time being. I see him coming with the bus shelter man in tow. They're slightly closer to the door than we are, but Shadow and I are quicker.

Following my lead, Shadow whirls around and rips back up the aisle. He loses his footing taking the turn toward the door, slides sideways down the steps and lands with a thump at the bottom.

The driver stomps his foot on the concrete to scare Shadow up and away. "Go on!" he yells. "Get out of here."

We fly around the front of the bus and down along the driver's side. Shadow's primed to keep running, but I call him in to wait out of sight around the back. I can hear the commotion playing out inside the bus.

"Is everyone ok? Where'd the dog go?"

"It took off over that way," someone says.

Expecting all eyes to now be turned out the windows on the driver's side, I quickly sneak Shadow up the other side and into the wide-open undercarriage. We shuffle our way right to the back between two suitcases. The commotion above dies down, and once the driver shuts both the doors and the bus takes off, Shadow is the perfect stowaway.

***

The decision to ride in the undercarriage is one that doesn't take long to regret. The floor is like corrugated rock, bags slide around and threaten to squash us with every turn, and the air is so stuffy that by the time the bus stops and the door is opened, breathing has become a luxury.

The exact number of hours Shadow and I spent in the undercarriage is anyone's guess. The diminishing oxygen levels have left us slightly delirious and incapable of caring who sees as we crawl from our hiding spot and fall out into the open air.

I don't know where we are, but it must be a long way from where we were, because the instant cold hits us harder and gets us moving a lot quicker than the driver's highly surprised, "What the? I thought I told you to...Go on. Get out of here."

Shadow manages to coordinate his feet enough to weave his way out of the busy bus exchange. We run until we are certain no one is chasing us, and when we stop to suck in all the air the bus trip deprived us of, I notice something ahead that instantly pinpoints our location. It's the iconic Opera House. We made it to Sydney.

***

On an average night, Sydney might be the most beautiful place on earth, but for Shadow and I, it's tainted by heavy rain clouds, bitterly cold, gusting winds, and the knowledge that it's still an incredibly long way from our intended destination.

We are stuck here. Deep in the heart of a frighteningly foreign concrete jungle, scampering past endless rows of tightly packed office blocks, grand Victorian style buildings and high-rises so tall they almost touch the stars.

Nobody stops to look at Shadow. A lonesome dog so out of place should surely draw somebody's attention, but everyone seems too busy to notice, too busy to care.

It's impossible for me to locate north, south, east, or west. Everything looks the same, and before we end up simply walking round and round in circles, I know I need to figure out how we're going to get out of here. At the moment, the best I can come up with is just keep walking. So that's what we do.

As if to make our big city experience even less welcoming, the clouds open directly above us and it starts to rain. The people around all rush for cover: some hide under their umbrellas and keep moving, others gather beneath cafe awnings or building entranceways to wait it out.

There's a small, dry gap between a pair of women in business suits under one of the awnings ahead. I lead Shadow over, but straight after he squeezes himself into the gap, he decides to shake the rain from his coat, and consequently sprays it all over the two women.

One of them jerks backwards and cries out, "Argh! My new suit," edging the other one to jump to the defence of her friend's tailored cotton. With a swift kick and a "Shoo! Stupid dog," she drives Shadow and I back out into the rain.

We don't bother trying to fit in anywhere else after that. Shadow was lucky the woman's pointed heel didn't leave more than a soon-to-be bruise. With nowhere to take him if he gets seriously hurt, I can't afford for someone else to do worse damage.

With no option but to ignore the rain, Shadow and I press on through street after sodden street. Eventually we navigate our way away from the city centre until the high rises are replaced with apartment buildings, and further along, houses.

The raindrops gather strength and soak deep into the hairs on Shadow's back. His coat turns a sad shade of mottled coal, and when I feel the blistering cold as though it were seeping into my own bones, I know we need to find shelter—and soon.

There's another empty bus stop a little further up. It's covered with graffiti, and I can already smell the stench of urine, but it has a roof and a bench seat to keep Shadow up off the wet ground, so it'll do.

Huddled together on the cold aluminium seat, we watch through the rain as cars stream by, sending sheets of water into the air and all over the already soaked pavement. The wind picks up and belts angrily against the flimsy walls of our shelter. It's almost as though it's yelling at us, just like the woman in the business suit, saying get out! You don't belong here.

It's a miserable end to an even more miserable couple of days.

I wrap my arm around Shadow, wishing I could take away

the shivering that stiffens his bones and cramps his muscles. I'm too afraid to look into his eyes. I don't want him to see the pity in mine. I don't want him to see how utterly uncertain I am about what to do next. I'm supposed to be his leader, but I am so completely lost. I can't communicate with anyone to ask for help. I can't even find him a decent place to sleep.

"I'm so sorry, Shadow." I squeeze him tightly through a new bout of shivering. "I'm sorry I'm failing you."

When Shadow looks at me, I see the same innocent optimism in his eyes that I see every time I begin to spiral downward. He fights through the shivering to keep eye contact, and once again, the picture he always seems intent on showing me finds its way into my mind: the quiet country road, Astrid, the feeling of euphoria...Mick.

The last two times I saw it, I could allow myself to believe it might be a vision, but with Mick gone, I know with certainty it's just wishful thinking.

***

Long after the cold and dark have chased even the raindrops from the sky, and too weary to have bothered hunting for a better place to sleep, Shadow and I lie cramped together on our aluminium bench shielded from the weather by three flimsy plastic walls and a skinny roof.

I watch the sky changing throughout the night from black to grey to pink. I watch the birds that line the roofs stretch their wings and take to their new day's activities. I watch the street as it welcomes the first of the morning's drivers and I feel the hunger as it drums Shadow from his sleep and announces itself ready to be stilled.

Aside from hungry, the hours of shivering have also left

Shadow as stiff as an old man. He almost falls when he tries to climb down from the bench seat, where he carefully stretches into shape while I take the time to properly survey our surroundings.

For the first time, I notice the sign on the side of our little bus shelter: Western Sydney University, Campbelltown.

"So we must be somewhere in the western suburbs," I tell Shadow, who's done with his stretches and is now limbered up enough to start the day. "I guess as long as we keep the morning sun on our left, once it comes up, we should be able to figure out which way south is." I try my hardest to sound positive. "We've made it this far. Things can only get better from here, right?"

27

Cut

After the leafy greens of the Western Sydney University campus, the Campbelltown golf course is the next thing to catch our eyes. It's a welcome little slice of country wedged neatly between the rows and rows of suburban houses and apartment blocks that dominate the area.

Having found nothing substantial for Shadow to drink since Olivia's house, the glassy sunrise-yellow water of the course's lake practically sings to us and I think that even if it were filled with sneaky crocodiles, we would still take our chances at a sip.

A 'temporarily closed' sign invites us onto the grounds and allows us to enjoy the squish of manicured lawns beneath our feet without fear of copping a golf ball to the head. At the lake, Shadow slides his front feet down into the water, where he thirstily laps around the small cloud of silt he inevitably stirs up. It's incredibly peaceful, even with the not-too-distant hum of traffic.

There are birds chattering away in the trees over by the empty clubhouse, a couple of frogs calling out to each other from the reeds that partly line the lake's banks, and an Asian woman dressed in a Cinderella-style bridal gown moping her way across the little wooden bridge in the middle...wait! What?

The woman is certainly a head-scratching sight. She makes it to the middle of the bridge, where she buries her face in her hands. Careful not to upset her glistening, bee-hive-style, jet-black hair, she buckles down into the layers of her dress, plonks onto her backside, and dangles her white-slippered feet over the bridge's edge.

Sobbing, perhaps a little over-dramatically, she removes a golf-ball-sized diamond ring from her finger, and with a gutsy cry that echoes across the water, tosses the ring into the cool.

It plops, with a comparatively light splash for its size, near Shadow's nose. Instead of sinking, the way a good diamond should, it takes to bobbing up and down like a sparkly plastic toy, catching not only the sun, but also Shadow's eye.

As if all of that isn't strange enough, especially for this early morning hour, a male's voice, sharp and frustrated, like a commanding officer just flown in from some US Naval base to enforce much needed discipline on a rogue troop, snaps from behind a hedge near the bridge's on-ramp.

"Oh, for god's sake! There's a goddamn dog in the water. Cut!"

I see the movie camera first. It pokes out around the hedge, held tight by a man with a neatly trimmed beard, a man bun, and way too little room to move in his tight grey polo and skinny black jeans.

The bride on the bridge bunches up her layers of tule to

stand unhindered. "Hey, look!" She points at Shadow with a laugh and an Aussie accent that makes me double check my initial Asian judgement. "He's playing fetch with the ring."

The man with the camera appears far less amused. "Adrian," he hollers across the lake, prompting another hedge on the opposite side to start rustling. "Adrian, get that dog out of the water, would you?"

The hedge rustles again. "I can't," a second male voice calls back, this one softer, more melodic, and ringing with New Zealand origins. "My nappy's stuck."

While I'm growing more intrigued by the minute, Shadow's plucked the ring from the water and is making his way up the bank again.

The bride watches him with hands on hips and a pretty smile that's tarnished by the scowl in her eyes. She turns her attention to Mr. Man Bun, flattening her smile. She then moves on to whoever's tucked behind the other hedge, dropping her mouth further to a frown. "I can't believe I got teamed up with you two idiots." Her words couple perfectly with her newfound facial disgust. "I could be with Sarah and Phillip right now, making a *proper* movie about *proper* multiculturalism, but *nooo*. I'm stuck here playing a Chinese bride who leaves her husband at the altar, at sunrise, because everyone gets married at sunrise. And then I meet and fall in love with an Aboriginal who's *so stupid* he got lost going walkabout. Tell me, Scott, what part of 'this is a joke' don't you understand?"

Scott must be the man with the camera because he's now using it as an excuse not to make eye contact with the bride.

"You're only supposed to play the part of a bitch, you know, Liu." He keeps his tone tight. "Not actually be one."

"I like to stay in character," The bride, Liu, retorts.

From the other hedge, I hear, "Oh, come on you two, don't start this again. The assignment's due in three weeks. We haven't got time for all this arguing."

Liu ignores the hidden man's attempt at peacekeeping, instead trying to drag him into her war. "What the hell are you doing there, Adrian?"

"I told you," he whines, "I'm stuck. My nappy's caught on this bush."

Scott makes a point of correcting the stuck Adrian. "It's not a nappy, you idiot, it's a loin cloth. God, you're just as bad at being Aboriginal as Liu is at putting on a Chinese accent."

"That's because I'm not actually Aboriginal." Adrian seems sorry for the truth. "You see, my mum's Polish, and my dad's Maori. And Liu doesn't even speak Chinese."

Liu backs Adrian up. "Exactly. Born here, Scott."

"Well," Scott holds firm, "you can at least *try* to put an accent on. You know, for the sake of the movie, and, ah, I don't know, maybe also because you want to be an actress?"

"Maybe if it was a proper movie," Liu bites back. "But it's not, is it, Scott? It's a university project, and a turd of a one at that. Luckily Mr. Creelman's the only one who's going to see it. Actually…" She pauses with one finger in the air. "Wait, where's he from again? Isn't he Scottish? Here's an idea. Why don't we give that dog over there a kilt and a set of bagpipes; that way we can be sure to insult *everyone*."

The elusive Adrian finally stumbles out from behind his

hedge. He's re-wrapping a bright orange loin cloth between his thighs and around his waist, which admittedly does resemble an oversized nappy. His skin is the colour of coffee with extra milk, and it's covered with spiralling, white finger-paint markings, none of which I imagine hold any researched significance. He brushes a leaf from his short-shaven head before turning to Shadow with a slightly buck-toothed smile. "Hey, buddy," he says, his voice way too soft for his warrior build, "can I have that ring back, please?"

I hear Liu on the bridge. "Pretty sure it doesn't speak English, Adrian."

Scott's set his camera up on a tripod and is now fiddling further with a fluff-covered microphone on a stand. "Don't worry about it," he says. "I've got three more. Just shoo the dog away so we can keep filming."

"Hey, guys?" Adrian's cocoa eyes glint. "Why don't we use the dog in the movie?"

"Are you serious?" Scott holds still to make sure he heard right.

Liu's, "Why not?" has more mockery painted on it than Adrian's non-Aboriginal skin.

She then launches into the most colourful spiel I think I've ever heard, only made better by an entire alphabet of tones, hand gestures, and facial expressions.

"I mean, my character goes walkabout through the Blue Mountains with a man who she already knows is useless with directions, and if that's not bad enough, then she goes out with him to Cocoparra National Park for a dip at Falcon Falls, which will most likely not only be dry this time of year, but also just as unspectacular as your upbringing out that way,

Scott. Which almost leads me to want to ask why on earth you want to film out there? I mean, your dad took your mum from America, all the way out to that godforsaken place, got her pregnant and had you, then beat the crap out of both of you because you turned out gay, which tells me you both left for a reason. Right? What would your mum say if she knew you were going back out there? Actually, no, don't answer that. I really don't know if I can sit through another one of your 'my sad childhood in Yenda' monologues. Anyway, back to our *riveting* movie. Somehow, after a stunning stint at Cocoparra, we all of a sudden find ourselves down on the Great Ocean Road looking out over the Twelve Apostles, one of which we half-walk, half-swim out to, climb up, and commit suicide off because society won't let us be together. And might I remind you, I have to wear this stupid cream-puff wedding dress for the entire movie. Walking, climbing, swimming: everywhere! How much worse could a dog make things? My dad always said if you're going to do something, do it right. So I vote, if we're so hell-bent on making this movie bad, we should go all the way and make it a *complete disaster*. The dog could be a guide that leads Adrian to me. It'll add a bit of drama because I'm Chinese, so everyone will be expecting me to eat it after we get lost and I start getting hungry."

"Oh, well, wow-ee!" Scott clearly doesn't appreciate Liu's recap of his life or her racial insinuations. "Who's being insulting now, huh?"

"I'm Chinese," Liu looks like she's having fun, "I'm allowed."

Scott, on the other hand: not so much fun. "Oh, I see." He speaks like a true cynic. "So, you're only Chinese when it suits you. Have I got that right?"

"That's exactly right, Scott."

"Liu," Scott calms himself, taking a deep breath, "you're a nightmare. You know that?"

"And you're a rotten director."

During all the arguing, Adrian has managed to escape everyone's attention and has made friends with Shadow. "Enough already!" He groans. "I've got the ring back, and look," he rests a gentle giant hand between Shadow's ears, "the dog's really friendly. I reckon we should incorporate it into the story. Like Liu said, it could be like a guide or something. I reckon that'd be pretty funny."

Scott is running short of deep, calming breaths. "Um," he collects himself, "aside from the fact that none of us know how to train a dog, we can't exactly just borrow someone else's dog and take it with us without asking. We're driving all the way down to Melbourne to the Great Ocean Road, remember?"

"Yeh, but only for a couple of days." Adrian doesn't see the problem. "Then we'll bring him back and drop him off here again, and he can go home."

"It probably doesn't even have a home," Liu joins in. "It doesn't have a collar or anything. I bet it's a stray. I'm with Adrian. I say we take it. It'll give me someone intelligent to talk to."

While Scott and Liu throw silent, snide-tipped daggers at each other, Adrian bares his bucked teeth again and asks Shadow, "Wanna be in a movie with us, little mate?"

It's a bit of a roundabout trip, I know. We'd have to travel with them out to however far away the Blue Mountains are, and then on to some national park I've never heard of, but the ending will be worth it. They're heading to the Great Ocean Road. Toward Melbourne, which I know is at least in the same state as Echuca. A couple of days of listening to the trio's arguments and we'll almost be at Astrid's. Only a fool would say no to that.

28

Movie stars and madness

It's a surprisingly short trip in the trio's mini van out to the Blue Mountains. I was expecting days, but I don't even think it was hours.

Scott's plan is to film Liu and Adrian standing, hand in hand, at some place called Lincoln's Rock Lookout, where they'll come across Shadow, who will then guide them out into the great unknown.

As much as I'd like to be proud of Shadow's part, Liu's right; this movie does seem like an embarrassing mess.

At the Lincoln's Rock car park, Liu complains about the two-minute walk to the lookout, and at the lookout, she complains about the view.

Making it out to the edge myself, I can't fathom how anyone could come here, regardless of the circumstances, walk out onto this football field of a rock, witness this view, and not be inspired. The mountains, rolling forward in every direction under the crystal-clear morning sky, are spread out as though each means to give the other their very own moment to shine. Carved, rocky outcrops jut above the ebb and flow of matchstick trees below, green tops blurring together like a cloak, blanketing everything from the tallest ridges to the deepest valleys.

It's so spectacular, I am almost able to lose myself in it enough to block out the sound of Liu, now loudly blaming Scott for everything from the blister on her heel to the fact that she forgot to bring her water bottle.

Scott's retaliation is a mumbling of profanities, and possibly the incorporation of a new scene in his film, one in which Liu might take a dive off the edge of Lincoln's Rock.

Adrian, on the other hand, seems to be a master of calm. He explains everything to Shadow as if he were any other person, telling him, "So you'll sit over there and then Liu and I will walk up that way."

Shadow listens to it all and sees all of the images I relay through, but there's none of the excitement like there was when dancing, or even just being with Mick. Everything from this point on is no more than a means to an end for both of us. The better he does his job, the quicker we can be on our way to the next location, and then on to our long-awaited destination, Melbourne – and eventually Echuca and Astrid.

***

Unfortunately, Shadow plays his part better than both Liu and Adrian, leaving us with a lot of waiting, and Scott with a permanent grimace of frustration.

By the end, Adrian's feet are so sore, from take after take of climbing up and down over rocks, that he's left hobbling back to the car park while Liu, who's proving to be the most unsympathetic person in the world, is saying, "Well, at least you won't have to spend the next two hours pulling prickles out of them, like I will with this dress."

"Five and a half hours," Scott bluntly corrects, ushering his crew of actors into the mini van before parking himself in the driver's seat. "It's five and half from here to Yenda. If you pull each one of those prickles out with your teeth, Liu, that'll give the rest of us five and a half hours of not having to listen to you."

"Are you kidding me?" Liu shrinks back as though she's just been spat at.

"Why would I kid about not wanting to be further subjected to your incessant whining?"

"No, you jerk, I mean are you kidding me with the five and a half hours business? I thought it was only, like, two or something." She slumps hard against her seat back. "Oh, God have mercy," she prays to the roof lining. "Why on earth did I say yes to this?"

"Stop it, guys," Adrian whines. "You're scaring the dog."

Both Liu and Scott turn to glare at Adrian, whose bucked teeth bite down on his bottom lip lending him a dopey appearance.

"What?" he asks. "I just don't see why you guys have to fight all the time. Can't you at least *try* to be civil? For mine and the dog's sake? *Please?*"

"Alright," Liu moans. "But if he," she jabs a thumb through the air in Scott's direction, "says one more word..."

"He won't." Adrian makes a weak promise on Scott's behalf. "We're all going to be stuck in this van together for a lot

longer than five and a half hours. Let's not kill each other before we get this movie done. Agreed?"

Liu's "Agreed" sounds anything but, while Scott's grunt
from the front seat leaves even more to be desired.

"Good," Adrian concludes, patting the seat beside him for
Shadow to jump up onto. "In that case, wake me up when we
get there."

As soon as Adrian falls asleep, Shadow relieves himself of
his bus-buddy duty to return to the seat beside me. After the
cold, hard, aluminium bench last night, and the rough, airless
trip down the day before, the inside of the mini van couldn't
be more appealing if its seats were made of silk.

Shadow follows Adrian into the Land of Nod, and soon
after, Liu loses her own battle with her eyelids, leaving Scott
to push the mini van on in silence toward the town of Yenda
and the memories of his, as Liu called it, sad childhood.

***

Scott says we're only a little over an hour out after he
wakes his passengers for a fuel stop. Liu rolls out of the mini
van in her prickle-covered wedding dress, snatches a bag
from under her seat, and heads off to find a restroom. She returns in jeans and a sweater, only to be turned away from the
mini van by Adrian, who's trying to scrub his finger-paint off
with a rag before getting dressed.

"How is it that you're only just doing this now?" she asks.
"Haven't you had, like, four hours to get that stuff off?"

"Yeh." Adrian sounds genuinely apologetic. "I fell asleep.
Sorry."

"Useless!" Liu mutters. "Well, I'm getting something to
eat. What time is it? Where's the other idiot?"

"He's in paying for the fuel. And I think it's about four-thirty. It'll be dark soon. Hey, do you know where we're staying tonight?"

"How should I know?" Liu seems to have woken up in fine form. "A hotel or something, I guess, in the raging town of Yenda, no doubt. If we're lucky we might even find one that's having a barn dance and we can spend the night doing the heel-and-toe and challenging the locals to an arm wrestle."

"What's the heel-and-toe?" Adrian's curious. "How do you do that?"

"I don't know. It's some old fogey's dance from back in the day when their musical instruments were bottle tops on sticks. I heard a friend's dad talking about it once: said they did it when he was in primary school, like a hundred years ago."

"You know," Adrian tries to politely slide his way around the lash of Liu's tongue, "I hope you don't plan to be this disrespectful if you *do* meet any locals when we get there."

"Disrespectful?" Liu does the best acting I've seen from her so far. "Me? Wouldn't dream of it. Hey, come to think of it, do you think they would ever have even seen a Chinese person out here?"

"You're unreal," Adrian answers, returning to his scrubbing, but it's clearly not a compliment. While Liu makes her way inside to find food, he wipes the last of the paint off, wraps himself in something warmer and more appropriate than a loin cloth, and ventures out to stretch his legs in the crisp country air.

Since Adrian is the only one even remotely interested in

Shadow, we follow him away from the fuel bowsers to the border of the same well-worn road we've been following since this morning.

He's both discouraged and inspired by the outlook. "Left and right lead into a whole lot of nothing," he says. "But I like the silence. Reminds me of being in the snow. It's like the whole world is padded, so every sound kind of stops where it starts. You know what I mean?"

With no clue what Adrian means, I don't have a hope of explaining it to Shadow. I don't think Shadow would care much anyway. Losing Mick has more than taken its toll; he's completely lost his spark. Though I'm certain he'll get it back once we make it to Astrid's, for the time being, he doesn't seem to want to be cheered up by anything.

The three of us bathe in the golden glow of the setting sun for a moment longer. No cars pass, giving Adrian nothing further to look at than the fluffy burgundy tops of the wild Natal grass lining the road.

"I love that stuff," he says. "Love how it looks in the sunset. Always looks beautiful in photos too. Man, it's peaceful out here."

Unfortunately the peace doesn't last long.

The jingle of bells rings all the way out to our ears as the petrol station's door is flung wide open. The bells are quickly drowned out by the sound of Liu and Scott who are, of course, at it again.

"You don't seriously think I'm staying in some cotton-eyed-Joe shack with your wife-bashing dad, do you? Is he even supposed to be out of prison?"

"He was never *in* prison, Liu! Oh my god, you're such a self-centred princess. Is your life really so perfect that you're now too good for everything: too good for me, too good for this movie? Did you ever stop to think about why you ended up with Adrian and I, instead of Sarah and Phil, like you wanted? I'll tell you why. It's because they didn't want *you*. No one did because you're too much of a cow. I'll tell you what, as soon as we're finished this, we're absolutely done. You're on your own after this, and good luck passing university and getting into the industry, when no one will work with you."

"Well, *I'll* tell *you* what." Liu's banshee shouting lures the petrol station attendant outside. "Why wait till the movie's done, Scott? If I'm *that* annoying, why put up with me a second longer?"

"Trust me," Scott, wary of the unwanted attention lowers his voice to a blade-sharp growl, "I wouldn't if I didn't have to."

"Then I've got great news for you." Liu smiles. "You don't have to. I'm out of here."

Pacing to the driver's side of the mini van, and not bothering to answer Scott's, "What do you think you're doing?" Liu wrenches the door open, swings inside, turns the key before slamming the door shut, and shudders the mini van into gear.

In a flash, Scott's beside her door trying his hardest to keep up as Liu kicks the mini van up to running speed. "Where do you think you're going?" he shouts, spraying spittle and hate all over the window. He tugs on the door handle with one hand and bashes his other against the glass, but both are closed and locked.

Refusing to let go, he allows himself to be dragged stumbling through the gravel, threatening, "All my gear's in there! You'd better stop this van right now, or I swear to God..."

Liu puts the pedal down and steers hard left, guiding the wheels into a sideways drift through the car park.

Adrian and I watch with horror as Scott is flung to one side amidst a spray of gravel and ultimately sent tumbling like a discarded rag doll into the same tuft of Natal grass Adrian had only just finished admiring.

Not bothering to check Scott's outcome, Liu fights the steering wheel for control, drifts further toward the road, and finally fishtails to a straight line in our direction.

Adrian, who until now couldn't bring himself to do much more than gape, decides he doesn't need a baton from his teammate Scott to start his own race. Pumping his legs into gear, he only just catches Liu as she pulls out onto the cracked bitumen.

"Waaaaiiittt!" he wails, swiping at the side door handle. "You can't leave me here. What did I ever do to you?"

Back on the gravel, Scott's made it to his knees. His jeans and polo are a little worse for wear, but I imagine the dirt will wipe off them quicker than it will his soul. He doesn't bother getting to his feet to chase after the mini van again. There wouldn't be any point from his position, but there is from ours, and unless we want to get left out here as well, we need to get back on that mini van when Adrian does.

Liu's seen Adrian in her mirror. Surrendering to his wailing, she takes her foot off the accelerator long enough for him to grab the side door handle. He reefs it open as Shadow and I start to run.

"Make sure you get in before he shuts it, Shadow!" I yell, watching Adrian sail feet first into the mini van better than an Olympic pole vaulter.

Adrian's upper body dangles dangerously outside the mini van, his head only just skimming the road. Shadow's right beside him on the ground, running and searching for a gap big enough to jump into. Liu turns to see if Adrian's inside yet, carelessly yanking down on the steering wheel at the same time, causing the mini van to swerve hard again to the left. The manoeuvre almost wipes Shadow out. Luckily on the ball, he only just manages to dash to the side before becoming the victim of a rear tire. Showing little interest in Shadow's safety, and only marginally more in Adrian's, Liu jerks the mini van back to the right, yelling over her shoulder, "Hurry up and get in, you idiot."

The whole scene resembles a bank robbery getaway. Adrian's clinging to either side of the door for dear life while Shadow's trying to find a way under, over, or beside him. Any way in will do. But Adrian's upper body is blocking the entire opening, and as he finally finds enough grip to pull himself all the way inside the mini van, Liu hits the gas again and Shadow is left behind.

"I'm sorry, dog," Adrian calls back to what he'd clearly hoped would be his new friend. "I'm really sorry."

"Shut the door!" I hear Liu's voice trail behind Adrian's.

Adrian does as told, keeping an apologetic eye on Shadow until the very last second.

We watch the mini van until it's nothing more than a tiny white dot on the horizon, then hang our heads and turn back toward the petrol station and the only person left that might know another way out of here. Scott.

***

The cloud of dust the minivan stirred up still sticks to the disbelief on Scott's face and coats the droplets of saliva that fall from Shadow's panting tongue.

The petrol station attendant doesn't seem to know who's side he should be on. His gaping grin implies 'you go, girl!' while the hand on the head feels more like a sympathetic gesture aimed at the newly abandoned Scott. "You alright, man?" he dares, keeping a cautious distance.

From what I've seen, Scott's had enough practice at deep breathing to out calm a monk, and right now I really wish he could pass a little of his composure onto me. Shadow and I are now stuck in the middle of nowhere with one road before us, facing west to who knows where and east all the way back through the Blue Mountains. Unless we stick with Scott, in the hope that he'll be kind enough to take Shadow back to Sydney (when he finds his own way, that is), it's going to be an awfully long trek getting out of this mess.

29

Dad's with guns

Scott's dad is a man of very few words. He answered and ended Scott's phone call for help in a frosty few seconds, then pulled into the petrol station car park sometime after dark, greeting his son with little more than a nod.

Three quarters bald, overweight around the middle, with a face that belongs in a maximum-security prison and a gap between his front teeth harbouring something that looks like a corn kernel, he doesn't come across as the kind of person I would usually want Shadow keeping company with.

Unfortunately, unless I want Shadow getting lost like a hiking tourist who forgot to bring a compass, we have to stay close to our only chance back to a secure path south. That chance is with Scott, and since Scott is taking his chances with his father, we're going to have to as well.

Scott isn't exactly enthralled by Shadow following him around the car park and over to his dad's car. Twice already I've heard him mumble, "I never should have let those idiots talk me into taking you. Now what am I supposed to do with you?"

At least he's considerate enough not to tell Shadow to get lost.

After his initial nod, Scott's dad stays seated quietly behind the wheel as we approach. He looks his son up and down, letting his eyes linger longer than usual on Scott's man bun and tight jeans. He doesn't need to say a word to convey his distaste.

"I see you're still gay then," is his hello as Scott opens the passenger door.

"I see you're still a drunk," Scott replies, moving an empty rum bottle off the passenger seat.

Noticing Shadow waiting behind Scott, his dad asks, "What's with the dog?"

Scott's answer, and every answer thereafter, is void of any care factor.

"It's a stray from in town."

"Looks purebred."

"Dunno."

"What are you gunna do with it?"

"Dunno."

I quickly tell Shadow to put his front feet up on the doorstep next to Scott's legs and to try to look friendly. He does as asked but there's still very little spark in his actions, which oddly seems to suit Scott's dad.

"Looks tough," he comments. "Throw him on the back seat."

Scott pushes Shadow down off the doorstep without so much as a smile. He gets out, opens the back door, waits while I slip in first and call Shadow onto the seat beside me, shuts the door and hops back in the front.

It'd be a lie to try and calm Shadow's obvious unease with an everything will be ok. There are two more empty rum bottles clinking together at my feet, the upholstery is scarred through to the foam in places by cigarette burns, and the stench of stale nicotine is making me wish someone would please open a window.

Scott's dad, who I just heard Scott address as John rather than Dad, is clearly not the kind of person who cares to look after things: not his car, nor his relationship with his son.

Scott's already pointed out the alcoholism and Liu refused to stay with him on the grounds that he's a wife-basher. Everything will be ok, would be a hard lie to convincingly pull off at this stage, so it comes as no surprise that Shadow doesn't believe me when I do let the words leave my mouth. But given how nervously we're both staring at the shotgun lying on the floor behind the front seats, what else could I say?

***

Yenda at night could be any other rural town anywhere in Australia. It's got a deserted main street, a couple of shop fronts whose original owners probably wore knickerbockers, and of course a quintessential town pub.

We drive through it in under a minute, continuing then on into the darkness. We pass the lit-up front face of a wine cellar building, turn left and right more times than I can count, then bounce our way down a pot-hole covered dirt road to a small farmhouse flanked by rows and rows of some kind of fruit trees.

Pulling up to such an isolated house is eerie enough. Being called out of the car and led by torch light around to a claw-scratched, wooden dog kennel, with what looks like dried blood spatters sprinkled up and down its panels, is worse. It's nightmare material and it has Shadow backing up in a big hurry.

Scott's dad, John, attempts to call Shadow toward the kennel. I can see a chain lying on the ground beside it. It's bolted into the house wall behind the kennel and it instantly reminds me of the old, abandoned dog Shadow and I once rescued.

Shadow's senses fly into overdrive. From his cowering position behind me, he stretches his twitching nose toward the kennel with unmistakable fear.

"Don't worry," I promise him, "there's no way on earth you're getting put on that chain."

The image I get from him in return is one in which we are running, sprinting as fast as we can away from this horror movie scene, out into the night to never return.

"Where are we supposed to go though?" I ask, replaying the long drive out here and the countless left and right turns in my head for him to see. "I wouldn't have a clue which way to run. I hate to say it, but we have to stay close to Scott. We have to be with him when he goes back to Sydney. I honestly don't know how we'll survive if we get stuck out here alone."

John interrupts our silent conversation. "Dog! Here!" He clicks his fingers to try and draw Shadow closer to the chain. Shadow backs further away.

"Here!" he says again, shorter and sharper than the first time.

Scott's standing beside his dad, watching Shadow with a look that says don't do it, dog.

He asks, "What happened to the last one?" flicking his head toward the blood-flecked kennel.

"Died."

"How?" Scott doesn't seem entirely sure he wants to know the answer.

"Shot him."

"Of course you did. Any wonder this one's not so keen on coming near you."

"We're not in the city now, boy." It sounds like a line John's used a time or two before.

He attempts to pass the chain to Scott. "Here. You put him on it then, since you seem to be the dog whisperer."

Scott keeps his arms firmly crossed over his chest and changes the subject. "Don't you even want to know why I'm here?"

"You told me on the phone already," John replies. "Your movie thing."

"Yeh, but... Doesn't it seem odd to you that I'd choose to film out here?"

"Not much about you that isn't odd, son."

Scott's right eyebrow briefly springs up, then his face falls blank as he obviously decides not to enter into battle. His next words are blunt. "Mum's sick: thought you should know in case there's any part of you that might regret not getting the chance to apologise."

John doesn't move for a minute. His face gives nothing away. He just stares at the chain in his hand, forcing us all to listen to the whistling of his bulldog nose as he breathes. "Right," he finally says, defaulting to an expressionless tone.

Without a further word, he drops the chain and heads into the house, taking Scott and the torchlight with him.

***

It was another miserable night for Shadow and I.

Not wanting to be stared at by the kennel and its blood stains, we found an old hessian sack lying in the dirt by the house's back door that, although stinking of mould, has so far managed to keep Shadow a little separated from the cold ground.

Not much sound came out of the house after Scott and his dad disappeared inside. Being such obvious polar opposites, Scott probably went straight to bed. I can't imagine what he would otherwise possibly stay up for and talk to his dad about. I certainly can't see the two sitting together having any kind of a father-son catch up.

Shadow's been too on edge to entertain the idea of sleep. He's spent the night nervously pinpointing every rustle in the surrounding fruit trees and every creak from the creepy, half-fallen down tin shed in the dark of the yard behind us.

We didn't even know the shed was there until a possum set a sensor light off. The possum was sneaking across the dirt behind the back of the house. The light surprised it from above the house's back door, sending it scampering back into the dark, but lighting up the shed. I wish it hadn't.

With a gaping black hole, in place of a door, surrounded by rickety sheets of rusted iron, it only adds to the horror movie appeal of this entire night. Instead of being stared at by a bloody kennel, I feel like we're being watched by whatever evil creature might reside in the shadows of that shed.

We shiver the hours away, curled into our hessian sack,

until the first grey of dawn starts to remove a little of the shed's creepiness. The new light reveals a bunch of garden tools slopped against the outer wall of the shed or thrown carelessly into the dirt in front.

There's something else on the ground there too. A small circle of jagged metal teeth lying right beside the doorway. Although I've never seen a claw trap in real life, I'm almost certain I'm looking at one now, and it looks like it's set. The sight of it makes me thankful the sensor light chased the possum away, and even more thankful Shadow and I were too afraid of the shed to venture anywhere near it.

***

By sunrise, my nerves finally loosen enough for Shadow to feel safe to attempt sleep. He's just fallen into a leg-twitching dream and I've just begun to unwind, when we are both jolted back into high alert by heavy, booted footsteps from inside the house and the sound of a glass being thrown against the floor. The smash is closely followed by what might be another rum bottle, this time hitting a wall.

I don't need to look through the one dust-covered window to know it's not Scott stomping toward the back door, and all of a sudden I feel a bit stupid for wasting so many good nerves on the shed. There was never anything to worry about in there. All this time, the real evil has been sitting inside the house, and judging by the way the back-door slams open and Scott's dad bursts through it, aiming a shotgun directly at Shadow's head, evil has been drinking up a storm.

"Hey, dog," he slurs through a grin fit for an insane asylum. "Wanna play fetch with a bullet?" Before either Shadow or I can even think to move, John does the unthinkable. He pulls the trigger.

30

Boo

I've heard everyone reacts differently to life-threatening fear. After our narrow escape from Greg and Sam, I thought I knew how I reacted – by running. But John pulling the trigger on Shadow is showing me a whole new side to myself that I never dreamed existed. I'm not scared, I'm not even upset; I'm *livid*. And I refuse to keep running.

The gun made no sound like it should have. In his drunken stupor, John didn't think to check if it was loaded, and as he sickeningly tells Shadow. "Wait there, dog. I've got bullets in the shed," I see beyond red. I see something angels probably shouldn't – revenge.

Shadow's filling my head again with the same images from last night, ones that show us running far, far away from this horrid place. This time I'm not listening. John needs to pay.

***

The stomping that happens next is no longer John's, it's mine. My body feels like it's grown into a fifty-foot-tall inferno of rage as I hunt John down on his way to the shed. There's no sense in my actions. Even with all my anger, John will never know I'm here, and by not telling Shadow to run, I know I'm putting his life further at risk. But for the moment, I'm too sick and tired of being afraid, to stop myself. I'm too outraged, by the grin I saw on John's face as he pulled the trigger, to think straight, and my body is too overcome by burning pins and needles to walk away without exploding.

John's just outside the shed when I catch up to him. He's stumbling and slurring a kind of singsong to himself: "Bullets, bullets...where did I put my bullets?"

He turns to see if Shadow is still where he left him. He isn't, of course. He's right behind me and I'm right behind John, seething like an angry giant who's ready to crush him with her bare fists.

John looks down at Shadow with the same crazed grin that initially set me alight. It adds fuel to the fire burning inside and it pushes the words out of me like a roar of flames engulfing a building. "How... Dare... You!"

I don't know what John hears, but his grin stiffens and he wobbles to a standstill. "Thought I heard something," he mutters, trying to hold himself straight on his feet. "Did you hear something?" he asks, loosely waving the barrel of the gun at Shadow again.

Shadow takes a couple of frightened steps back.

John laughs, so I take a couple of furious steps forward, and this time when I roar, it comes out as though I've just reduced the building to ash and am now ready to take on an entire city. "HOW...DARE...YOU!"

Instead of just his grin, John's entire body stiffens. In an instant, both hands are wrapped around the gun.

Like a soldier who's been ordered to aim, he swings it up until the butt is pressed firmly against his shoulder and the barrel is pointed right between my eyes. "Who's there?" he asks, his voice as nervous as his inebriation will allow.

He shifts his red-veined eyes left and right, following them with the gun and squinting to protect his dilated pupils from the morning sun. He lifts his tone to a pitchy, frightened shout. "I said – who's there?"

Just like Claire once revelled in Shadow's fear, I feel the empowerment that John's fear lends me. I know I'm out of control. I know I should take Shadow and run, but John's only one step away from his very own, cruelly set claw trap, and I can't think of any better way to ensure he doesn't make it into the shed for his bullets.

He swings the gun back in my direction. "Who's there?" he asks again. "Who's talking?"

I lean in beside the gun and breathe in the alcohol fumes pluming out of John's open mouth. I look him dead in his beady little burnt-pea eyes, knowing that one more word from me and he'll stumble backward into a world of agonising pain.

I should walk away now; he's frightened enough to have forgotten his former intentions. I don't. Instead, I lean just a little closer until I can almost kiss his foul, wet lips, and from there I whisper the one word that, as a ghost, I believe I'm entitled to.

"Boo!"

***

John took that last step backward.

The second the claw closed around his booted foot, stabbing its metal teeth through the leather and into the skin below with a sickening snap, I knew what I'd done was possibly going to keep me locked out of heaven for good. But Shadow was safe and that was worth any damnation.

John's screaming brought Scott out of the house. After he'd wiped the sleep from his eyes, he tore back inside to call an ambulance.

By the time he returned to his dad's side, John had already passed out from the mixture of pain, shock, and alcohol. Scott spent his time, while waiting for the ambulance, calling his dad a stupid drunk. He didn't have to do it for very long, which told me there must be a hospital reasonably close by.

I'd hoped that once the ambulance took John away, Scott would get in his dad's car and drive back to Sydney, taking Shadow and I with him, but Scott decided to only look after himself.

He asked the paramedics for a lift into wherever they were headed, saying he'd catch a bus from there, and despite the show I made Shadow put on, he was out-muscled by the paramedics who refused to let him into their sterile wagon.

It left us where we are now, somewhere on a pothole covered dirt road, with Yenda behind us, the morning sun on our left, and a whole lot of uncertainty laid out in front.

"No more people," I tell Shadow, "especially drunken farmers. I've seen what I'm capable of now. I don't want blood on my hands if someone else tries to hurt you."

Shadow's lightened since leaving John's. He seems content for us to go it alone from here, and I know from the pictures running through his head that the only person he'd stop for now is Mick. Of course, seeing Mick again is nothing more than a hopeless dream, and unless the days ahead bring more luck than those behind us, there's every chance that seeing Astrid again might become one too.

31

The harvester

We left Yenda with the decision made to no longer engage with strangers unless absolutely necessary. For a while, we stuck mostly to dirt roads and walked only under the cover of darkness or the thick blankets of fog that rolled in during the early morning hours to bury the world in a haze of white. While the plan did keep us hidden, it consequently also kept our main navigational tool - the sun - hidden from us.

I'd hoped the moon would at least come to our rescue, but on the first night it waited until dawn to rise. Even then it was only the tiniest sliver of white in the sky and was swallowed almost instantly by the building fog. It was of no help at all.

The nights after that, it didn't bother to rise at all, leaving me with no choice but to mark the sun's position while Shadow slept during the day, and then attempt to remember it in the dark. The strategy worked until we met with a T-junction somewhere around night six or seven.

Disoriented by the flat farming land all around, I chose

a direction that unfortunately lead to a dead end. I turned Shadow around and we retraced our steps as best we could in the near pitch black, but a hidden road fork sent us down an entirely new path and we never found our way back.

Instead, we landed on the edge of an unexpected bitumen road complete with white lines and guideposts that glowed every now and then in the headlights of infrequent passing cars. To go left or right was a complete guess. I chose left, and by the time the sun rose again, it did so directly behind us. We had spent the entire night heading west.

The next morning, we reverted back to traveling by daylight. We opted to take our chances away from the road, crossing sheep-filled paddocks with grass so green it could have been spray-painted on, and skirting our way around rice fields we didn't dare enter due to the giant harvesters working in them. They were devouring everything in their paths.

That was three days ago.

Since then, we have blindly followed the skinny water canals that border each of those rice fields. They're providing for Shadow's thirst, but they're also leading us in a maze of directions, taking us further and further away from any hope of finding food.

Our current count of days without food stands at four. Five if we leave out the discarded fried chicken wing Shadow found before we veered off the road, and six since the last substantial meal that came out of a tipped over roadside rubbish bin just outside of Yenda. It's no wonder the field mice being frightened out of their burrows by the rumble of a nearby harvester are now making Shadow drool.

Like headless chickens with an impulse to run, but no

thought put into which direction, they scatter both away and toward danger. Some try climbing the rice plants, only to have them bend under their weight and bring them straight back to the ground. Others seek refuge in burrows just abandoned, while others still are too distraught to move.

Shadow watches with an eagle eye as they dart in and out of the first row of crops in the field beside us. When one makes the decision to halt for a twitchy second near his front foot, Shadow's hunger takes over and he swoops down for his chance at a meal.

The mouse's reaction is quicker than Shadow's. Before his snapping teeth can get close enough to be of any threat, it scurries off into the field, running blindly away from one danger, but putting itself straight in the path of another: the oncoming harvester.

With his sights locked and tunnel vision blocking out everything, including my frantic cry to stop, Shadow takes off after the mouse. He bounds headlong into the field, nose down. He neither hears nor sees the harvester less than a small car's length behind him, leaving me standing like a useless lump of petrified wood with nothing to do but watch the unfolding tragedy.

Losing sight of Shadow amongst the hip-high crops, I shoot a glance up to the harvester's driver. It's a middle-aged woman sitting in a glass enclosed cabin, high up above the spinning auger and scissor-sharp cutters savagely chomping through the field in front. I wish I could say she'd surely see Shadow and stop, but she's got her head turned down and seems to be distractedly fiddling with something beside her seat.

Even more than that, I wish I could tell myself it wasn't a yelp I just heard coming from directly in front of the harvester's blades, but my frazzled-by-terror brain doesn't have the current capacity to pretend, and the sound instantly brings my panicked hands to my head.

I want to cover my eyes before the grain shooting out of the harvester's spout turns red, before I have to bear witness to Shadow being turned into rice-sized pieces. A second yelp brings me out of my state of shock and gets me moving. It was further ahead of the harvester than the first. Not *safely* far ahead, but a second-or-two-to-spare far.

"Shadow!" I shout over the deafening rumble of machinery, racing with the speed of desperate hope toward the yelp. "Shadow, where are you?"

I see the rice plants a few rows in front of me rustle as something moves through them. "Shadow, is that you?"

I hear another yelp, followed by a flash of grey.

"Quick, Shadow. Here!"

The harvester's catching up. We need to get out of its way, but Shadow's moving painstakingly slowly. Why isn't he running?

"Shadow! Get here now," I demand, at the same time making my way further through the field toward him.

I don't notice the pain in my leg until I break through to Shadow, but as soon as I see him limping and my eyes fall on the trail of blood behind him, it's there. I feel the throbbing from my ankle all the way up to my knee and the sting of each bladed leaf that scrapes past, as if we aren't surrounded by rice plants, but scalding hot irons.

Shadow's hurt. I can feel it as though it's my own wound, and it's not good.

"How could you be so stupid," I scream at him, but there's no time for my anger. The harvester is still boring down on us and we're both dragging wounded legs. The verbal lashing will have to wait.

With Shadow on three legs and me down to one, we limp as fast as we can along the clean, soiled row between the rice plants, trying to get as far ahead of the harvester as possible. Its cumbersome size keeps it at a steady distance, allowing us just enough time to find a gap in the thick of the crops which paves our way out of danger to the edge of the field.

We break through to the bordering canal under a cloud of dust spewed out from the back of the harvester. When the dust comes to rest, it coats everything, from the water in the canal to Shadow's hair, and on closer inspection, I also notice how it sticks to the blood pouring from his wounded leg.

It's not spurting, which I believe means he hasn't damaged an artery, but the flesh is cut through from the crease above his paw to halfway up his leg. I also can't tell if the white I'm seeing under all that blood is bone, cartilage, muscle or what. All I know is blood loss combined with hunger and exhaustion can't be a good mix.

"You need to elevate it," I tell him, knowing nothing about medical practices, but understanding the logistics of blood enough to realise it flows downward. "Wash the dust off first and then roll on your back."

Shadow chooses to lick the wound clean rather than climb down into the canal. Watching, I honestly don't know how he does it. The thought of licking up that amount of my own blood makes me want to vomit, but he doesn't seem phased by the taste. Once he's satisfied there's no more grit to be tongued out, he does as I show him and rolls onto his back, leaving his wounded leg to flop over his belly like a spare part.

It's a long afternoon and an even longer night of fretting. Thoughts of infection and gangrene almost see me giving in to the lure of a distant farmhouse's lights, but when I suggest to Shadow that we investigate in the hope of meeting someone kind with a bandage to spare, he reminds me of John and then shows me his leg. It's stopped bleeding.

"How did it happen?" I ask him, realising I had only made assumptions.

He shows me him running after the mouse and looking up to notice the harvester almost on top of him. I see the pointed blades as though they are only inches away from my own foot and I feel the slicing pain as his leg gets caught. He only just managed to pull it away before it was chopped off completely.

With no idea where we are, and presumably still such a long way to go, I can't help but finally let the anger erupt. Shadow could have been killed. It's time for a good talking to.

32

Barrow Station

The days that have followed our close call with the harvester have reduced my brain to a muddy cesspool of fear, uncertainty, and regret.

Shadow's leg bleeds, then dries out, then he licks it, and it bleeds again. The pain is manageable as long as he doesn't put too much weight on it, but the limping is keeping us from covering any great distance in a respectable amount of time.

We made our way as far from the crop fields as we possibly could, turning them into paddocks, and the canals into a very lucky amount of creeks. This means Shadow's thirst is taken care of, but food is becoming an increasing issue and it's showing on Shadow more than I want to admit.

For ages now, we've encountered nothing but grass, sheep, more grass, and more sheep. Oh, and a never-ending supply of flies. They've been buzzing around Shadow's wound for so long that he's given up trying to chase them away. I just hope they don't lay maggots in it. I don't want his leg ending up like the rotten bone he ate at Claire's before she took my shoe away.

***

Darkness rolls around again and for the fourth night in a row we are left with little to do but stare up into the velvet-black sky with its trillions of stars. It's as beautiful as it is lonely, and just like the night's before, its vastness makes us feel as though we're not on earth anymore, but lost somewhere deep in space.

The cooler days have brought a brilliant clarity to the air. There's no heat haze shimmering into the atmosphere to dim or interrupt the star's shine, so they don't even twinkle.

There are more constellations than I'll ever know the names of. While some sit high overhead, others appear so low, it's almost as though they're not in the sky at all. One particular cluster has caught my attention. It's about ten or so bright stars and is close enough to Earth to be disorientating.

The longer I stare at it, the more I notice how different it is from all the other clusters. Its individual lights are a warmer white. They're brighter, but somehow softer as well, and if I'm not mistaken, I think a couple of them just moved. I don't think they're stars at all. I think they're actual lights. Lights mean people, and if I cross enough fingers and toes, then maybe this time people will mean help.

Sore, tired, and hungry enough to understand he needs help, Shadow follows me as I'm drawn like a moth to a flame toward the lights.

We duck under a barbed wire fence and limp through another paddock, keeping a wide birth from a sleeping flock of sheep so as not to disturb them. A second fence lands us on a dirt driveway beside a simple, white sign boasting the words 'Barrow Station' in black block letters.

Since there's no trains out here, and I can't imagine too many buses would run this way either, I'm tipping we've stumbled onto a sheep station. There would have to be a few people living and working here, maybe even a vet. At the very least, there must be someone with a first aid kit.

It takes a lot longer to reach the lights than I thought it would, long enough to have me believing I might have mistaken their earthly origin. Thankfully they turn out to be every bit as real as the sheds and houses they shine down on and out of.

We snoop around the three huge sheds first. One is stacked to the ceiling with hay, one keeps an assortment of machinery out of the weather, and the third is closed up as tight as the maze of stockyards erected beside it.

Beyond the sheds, we find a large farmhouse. Its brick walls have windows along the entire front. Even with all those windows shut, the smell of a roast can't be contained. It's so strong, it's crippling, and both Shadow and I are forced to a standstill by the pains in our stomachs.

I see Shadow's intentions roll through my head. He's thinking of just walking right up to the front door and howling until they let him in and feed him. In a perfect world, it would be as simple as that, but as skinny and wild looking as Shadow is at the moment, there's a chance he could be seen as a threat to whoever comes to that door. After meeting John, I can imagine exactly how a concerned farmer might deal with such a threat.

"Just wait," I tell him, wishing I'd spent the walk here coming up with a plan. "I'd really like to know who we're dealing with before you show yourself."

Another wave of the roast aroma hits us hard enough to make us feel faint. I don't know for how long I'll have Shadow's attention while that smell is in the air, so I urge him on to a second house a little further down. It's a smaller version of the first house: brick walls, pitched roof, and windows along the front.

Outside the wide-open front door, there's a pile of dusty boots that look like they've been kicked off in a hurry and left to lie where they landed. Above the boots, a coat rack has been taken over by cowboy hats. Either side of the rack is framed by windows looking into individual single-bed rooms. This must be the staff's living quarters.

The sizzling sausage smell coming from a kitchen somewhere inside isn't nearly as overpowering as the roast, but together with the sound of country music and excited chatter floating out through the open door, the overall vibe is a lot more welcoming.

"Should we take a look?" I ask Shadow.

Shadow answers by leading the way up to the concrete landing.

We hear a female voice yell out from inside the house, "Are you ready yet, Sal?"

The sizzling gets louder: it sounds like sausages being turned over.

"Nearly," a second female answers. "Just waiting on these."

"You know there's food there, yeh?" the first one says.

"Yeh, but it's gunna take like an hour to get to Booroorban to pick Crazy up. Then it's a half-hour from there to Hay. I'll have faded away to a shadow by then. Did you put the swags in? Are the boys ready?"

"Yeh, we're all waiting on you."

Footsteps clunk out of one of the rooms, belonging to a guy dressed in a light blue vintage tuxedo with one of those t-shirts underneath that's supposed to make him look like he's wearing a bow tie.

"Bangers ready yet?" he calls to the girl in the kitchen, turning his head away from Shadow and I at the front door as he passes.

"Yeh, Dave," she answers, turning the sausages again. "I reckon so. Here, grab some for the road. Geez!" She pauses for a second, possibly to admire the guy's blue suit. "You scrub up alright. Who's grave did you have to dig up to find that thing? You look like my grandad in his wedding photo. Don't know if you should have your boots on inside though."

"My feet were cold." Dave quickly changes the subject. "You should see Dylan. He's wearing the same tux from last year."

"Didn't that thing get covered in blood from when that bloke tried to knock him out?" Sal in the kitchen wants to know. "Remember? He was dancing with that chick and her fella got jealous?"

The memory makes Dave laugh. "He never washed it either. Pretty sure there's still some vomit on it too."

"Oh my god, that's gross." Sal's voice has a hefty amount of cringe in it. "Glad *you're* sitting in the car with him. Hey, Jules," she raises her voice, "snags are up."

The first girl, dressed even more interestingly in a turquoise bridesmaid's-type dress with puffy sleeves and a giant satin bow stitched on one hip, flits past Dave. "Yeh, righto," she says. "Wrap 'em in some foil or something: just come on! I wanna get there before Zoe has a chance to get her claws into Trent."

"Ok, ok, I'm coming. Go and fire the utes up. I'll wrap these up, chuck my boots on, and we're outta here."

Jules, in the turquoise dress, comes back into view. Grabbing Dave by the arm, she pulls him toward the front door, where she stops so abruptly at the sight of Shadow standing just outside that Dave has no choice but to run into her.

"Oh, look out," she says, toppling forward with a surprised grin on her face. "We've got a visitor. How do you reckon it got here without setting the others off?"

"Must not have come past the kennels," Dave answers. "Geez, look at its leg!"

Sal, from the kitchen, pushes through from behind. Also in a dress, hers burgundy red, covered in sequins and pulled tight around her waist by a length of frayed twine, she points a half-eaten sausage at Shadow and speaks around the other half. "Where'd it come from?"

"No idea." Dave sounds no less baffled. "It's done well to get here though, with that leg. Give it a sausage. See if it's friendly."

"Wouldn't be standing there if it wasn't," Sal decides, tossing her half-sausage toward Shadow.

As quick as if he's frightened it'll grow legs and run away, Shadow snatches the sausage off the floor and gobbles it up. I tell him to wag his tail so that Sal will hopefully give him another one. He does as told, but Sal doesn't seem to want to part with any more food.

"Don't be so mean," Jules prompts, noticing her friend's

reluctance to offer another sausage: "Look at the poor thing." She pries the foil packet from Sal's hand. "It can have mine. I'm not hungry anyway."

One after the other, Jules hand feeds Shadow three more sausages that each disappear quicker than she can pull the next one from the packet.

"Don't give it all of them," Sal complains. "I didn't slave over a hot stove all afternoon just for some mangy dog."

"All afternoon?" Dave laughs. "You threw them on before you got in the shower and took them off when you got out." He reaches over Sal and pulls another sausage out for Shadow. "It can have mine too."

"That's the last time I cook for you lot." Sal fails miserably at sounding seriously cranky. "Should we tell the boss?"

Jules and Dave swap a glance that doesn't have a whole lot of confidence in it.

"Probably not." Jules says. "Probably be better off taking it with us to Crazy. She did that vet nurse course, remember? Maybe her parents will feed it up and keep it as a pub dog."

"You reckon Crazy's the best person to take it too?" Dave intervenes. "You do know why she never finished that course, hey?"

"Didn't she give a cow the wrong needle or something?" Jules tries to remember.

"Right needle," Sal corrects: "wrong cow though. Put a prize bull down."

Jules's face breaks into a guilty smile. "Oh, you're kidding!"

"Can you imagine?" Sal gets the giggles.

"Hence why she now works for Mum and Dad at the pub," Dave explains.

"Ah!" Jules nods. "I did wonder why she went back there. Well," she diverts back to Shadow, "what do you's reckon? We can't leave him here. The boss'll find him for sure, and I can pretty much guarantee he won't be interested in fixing the leg of a stray dog."

"Just throw it in the back of the ute," Dave suggests. "We'll see what Crazy says when we get there. It's got a better chance with her than it does here anyway."

"Have you guys got room in yours?" Sal asks. "Ours is full with the swags and stuff. Speaking of, where's Dylan?"

"He's been waiting in his ute. Knowing him, he's probably fallen asleep," Jules says.

"Well," Sal closes the door, passes a cowboy hat from the coat rack to each of her friends, and pulls on one of the pairs of dusty boots, "shall we?"

She starts ahead with Dave, leaving Jules tripping on her own boots to catch up.

"Come on, dog." Jules waves Shadow along toward the sound of car engines winding over and revving up. "If you want more sausages, you'd better hurry up."

33

Utes

Four and half sausages proves a tiring meal for Shadow. His shrunken stomach works overtime to digest them all, taking every last scrap of his energy and leaving him with the desire to do nothing more than close his eyes and rest; but the utes are ready to be driven away, and Jules's comments about their boss suggest we really should be in the back of one of them.

I have no idea where the places are that the girls mentioned – Booroorban and Hay – nor do I have a clue why they're all dressed like an eighties revival band. They must be headed to some kind of country-style party. If so, it's one with a really odd dress code.

Taking Shadow to a failed vet nurse called Crazy is somewhat off-putting, but so far no one has tried to hurt him, and staying here won't get us any closer to Astrid. Basically, all of that together leaves the decision made: we're going for another drive.

The two utes idling in the driveway are certainly attention-grabbing. One's red, the other's white, and that's the only normal thing about either of them.

Sal is behind the wheel of the red one. She's accidentally clamped her dress in the door, leaving the bottom half of it hanging out where it'll end up dragging along the ground. The hood has a silver statue of a rearing horse bolted onto it in the middle. In front of that, there's a bull bar so big it's making the car look like it's doing a nose dive, and attached to the bull bar are two long, flimsy aerials shuddering violently with each vibration of the engine. Behind her, a set of roll bars stands over a tray that's jam packed full of rolled up swags, eskies, fold-up chairs and backpacks. The tailgate of the tray has stickers plastered all over it; the kind tourists pick up at souvenir shops to show where they've been. Only Sal's stickers don't seem to be from famous holiday spots, but rather from pubs and places called Deni Ute Muster and Jerilderie Bachelors and spinsters ball.

The white ute, the one whose driver I'm guessing is the sleeping Dylan, puts Sal's to shame in terms of eccentricity. His has more stickers than paint, his bull bar is bigger, he's got a total of *six* aerials all up, and for some very strange reason, there's semi trailer exhaust stacks in between his cab and roll bars. They look like the ones on Mick's truck: just as big, just as loud, and breathing just as much smoke.

I can't decide if I love it or hate it. I *am* extremely impressed by the amount of lights on the ute though. There are so many little white ones set into the bottom of the panelling on all four sides that it reminds me of Christmas.

Dylan's wide awake, doing the whole revving thing while

Jules jumps in with Sal, who's already singing along at the top of her lungs to a song blaring through her radio. It's another country song with lyrics dedicated to utes and burnouts.

"Hurry up!" Jules shouts over the music to Dave. "What are you doing? It's gunna be too late to go soon."

"Won't get good till ten," Dave shouts back from behind Dylan's ute. "I'm trying to make room for the dog. Has anyone got a collar?"

"Just throw it in and tell it to hang on," Jules answers. "She'll be right. Come on, I've gotta get to Trent before Zoe does."

Dave pulls the tailgate down and pats the tray for Shadow to jump up.

"Don't!" I stop Shadow before he can even think about trying. "You'll open your leg up even more. He needs to lift you up."

With a whimper, Shadow beckons Dave for some help.

"Oh, yeh, sorry." He looks at Shadow's leg. "My mistake: come here then."

Lifting Shadow up and slamming the tailgate shut behind us as we nestle in between two swags, Dave runs ahead to the front and jumps in with a terribly Texan accented, "Yee-ha! Let's hit the road." He barely gets his door closed before Dylan puts his foot down.

The back wheels spin fast enough to burn the rubber off before the car even moves, spraying dust and rocks that could take an eye out if anyone were standing behind.

Seeing Dylan's actions as a challenge, Sal just about revs the motor off her own ute, prompting Jules to hang her head out the window and holler, "Catch us if you can, suckers!"

From there, the race is on.

***

I remember one of the girls saying it was an hour to Booroorban, but with the way Sal and Dylan are driving, I'll be surprised if it takes even a quarter of that. Skinny dirt roads, where the outside wheels of both cars hang over onto the grass, don't deter either of them from trying to drag ahead of the other. Corners neither of them could possibly see around without x-ray vision become drift opportunities, and bumps so big they bounce Shadow and I up into the air only succeed in making them drive faster.

It's a hairy ride, to say the least. I'd much prefer Shadow and I strapped in the front and wrapped in bubble-wrap, instead of careening from one side of the tray to the other, freezing cold air whooshing past and making our eyes water.

Sal seems to know the road better than Dylan. He takes a turn a little less daringly, giving her the edge to shoot out in front. It clearly doesn't sit well with him, because almost immediately he drops a gear and pushes his ute up close enough behind hers to nudge it.

Another bump in the road sees Shadow flying up from in between the swags and landing with a thud against a toolbox down near the tailgate. His bad leg is the first thing he lands on, causing pain to shoot through both of us and the bleeding to start again. His yelp gets lost in the wind as he tries to find his footing and scramble back up front.

"Lie down!" I yell at him. "Try to find something to bite down on so you can hang on."

While Shadow's yelping trails off, heard only by the animals in the paddocks behind us, I hear another voice flow through from in front. It's loud enough to be understood. Just one short, sharp word that I think comes from one of the girls. "SHEEP!"

I turn to see the taillights of Sal's ute swerve heavily to one side. With far more control than I remember Liu doing in the mini van, she fishtails back on to the road and the lights disappear in a cloud of dust.

I hear Dylan's horn blast, but like Sal, there's no slowing down, and before Shadow can find anything to grip, our ute takes a dangerous dive away from the road, hits another bump that flings Shadow into the air again, then swerves out from under him before he falls back down.

Instead of landing back in the tray, Shadow hits the ground hard. I feel the impact, the way it knocks every bit of air out of his lungs. His body tumbles uncontrollably into the grass and comes to rest in a small gully that's thankfully lined with mud, not rocks. He's too badly winded to yelp. Bruised from head to toe, he lies there for a terrifying moment, trying his hardest to suck in any amount of breath he can.

Nobody, outside of myself and the road-hog sheep that baas a couple of times before running off to find its flock, notices a thing. The taillights disappear, the sound of revving engines fades, and the dust settles. Shadow finds his breath and staggers to his feet. He's hurt, disorientated, trembling with shock, and we're right back where we started - in the middle of nowhere. But he's still alive.

***

I can count the good luck we've had on this trip on one hand. We met Rosie and George, found Mick, met Little

Olivia. The bad luck I would almost need to take my shoes off to count, if I were wearing any.

So far, Shadow has almost been turned into crab-pot bait, Mick died, we got kicked off a bus, were left stranded by the worst actress ever: Shadow's been shot at, run over by a harvester, fallen out of a ute, and to top it all off, we are once again completely lost.

Surely it's time for things to turn back in our favour.

34

The last rest stop

By my calculations, the utes left us somewhere between completely lost and never getting out of here alive. We didn't bother trying to move before daylight. Shadow slept where he landed, and has now woken up in such agony that I can't believe he's willing to move at all.

I feel every painful breath he takes, through what I suspect to be at least one cracked or broken rib, and I'm fairly certain it was concussion that caused him to throw up the only meal he's had in days.

He's not in a good way, which makes the fact that he refuses to give up, so much more impressive.

I suggest waiting it out for a day or so, gathering energy and seeing if the pain goes away, but the picture in Shadow's head says no. It's the same image he's shown me time and time again, the one of Astrid, the country road, and Mick. The one I think even he now knows is pure fantasy, and maybe only clings to as a way of keeping himself moving. So we move. It's slow and it hurts beyond belief, but somehow, we manage it.

We follow the same dirt road the utes took until some-time around midday, when we reach a fork and have to make a decision. Neither path appears any more main-route-like than the other, but the one on the right meets a little further up with a snaking line of trees, the kind that usually borders water. It's the first water we've come across since the muddy gully Shadow landed in, and it's more than enough to make the decision for us.

The tree line doesn't disappoint. The creek it shades quenches our thirst, rinses the caking blood from Shadow's leg, and offers a place for him to rest for a couple of hours. The afternoon is getting on by the time he's ready to ease into action again, and although I can feel his head spin from the effort of standing up, at least he's managed to keep the water down.

Like the car accident victims that we are, we limp, wheeze, wince and groan our way into a sunset that would usually be worthy of a thousand photos.

It closes in on the horizon to our right. At least that means we're heading south. As the bottom of it begins to sink into the earth, it silhouettes something even more out of place in this wide-open country landscape than Shadow and I – sculptures.

They're still too far away to figure out what they're depicting, and they're a little off course to the west, but the fact they're there is odd enough to make me want to investigate them.

We veer away from our dirt road and hobble into another wire-fenced paddock. We dodge cow paddies as if they were land mines and eventually come across a couple of paddy-dropping culprits. They decide to follow us all the way to the next fence line and moo longingly after Shadow when we leave them there. It's as if they can't quite remember what they were doing before Shadow came along.

On the other side of the fence, the grass is once again land-mine-free, and the sculptures are finally close enough to be more than just odd-shaped silhouettes. There's four of them mounted high up on individual poles and formed from some sort of rusted metal. There's two men on horseback herding a small head of cattle. Between them are a couple of dogs with the same heeler shape as Shadow, and behind everyone, there's a third rider. This one has a long cape blowing out behind him. He's holding a lantern in front, wielding a stock whip in his other hand, and for some reason, he doesn't appear to have a head.

There's a couple of plaques beneath the sculptures, and as I let my eyes fall further, I notice something else that I couldn't see through the grass and blinding sun...bitumen. We've found a main road.

As if to welcome us back to civilisation, the familiar rumble of an oncoming engine hits our ears. It's the exact sound we heard before we first saw Mick's truck and it stupidly makes my heart skip a wishful beat.

Shadow's head flies up and he glues his eyes in the direction of the noise. For a second, I think of his image: the quiet country road, Mick...maybe he didn't die after all. But there's no Astrid here, and the closer the truck gets, the easier it is to see it's nothing like Mick's. It's blue, for a start.

It scoots past, without so much as a blink from the driver,

and carries on down the white-lined road until it's nothing more than a glint in the last rays of sunlight.

With no further traffic to be seen or heard, Shadow and I cross over to the sculptures for a hopeful understanding of where in the world we are.

The plaque beneath the sculptures reads: The Headless Horseman. It tells the tale of drovers and their cattle being spooked by a man who died at a nearby Black Swamp. It isn't of nearly as much interest to me as the bunch of signs at the other end of what appears to be a rest stop. They explain we are on a trail called the Long Paddock, which means nothing to me, but the fact that it runs from somewhere called Wilcannia to Moama means everything.

Astrid had talked about driving into Moama often enough for me to know it isn't far from her. Just across the border, I remember her saying, and the memory of those words is enough to begin to lift the weight of uncertainty off my shoulders.

"We're on our way, Shadow. This is the road that's going to lead us home."

***

Knowing we are finally on the right path has me wanting to keep walking straight away, but one glance down the isolated road ahead tells me our rest stop's little picnic table might be the last form of shelter we see for a very long time. It could also be one of the only places where any passing traffic might slow down enough or actually stop to help us. For those reasons we decide to wait the night out before moving on.

We scavenge through the rest stop's rubbish bin for food,

but outside of a few bits of paper, a bottle top, and a blackened banana peel, it's empty. I feel Shadow's concussion, or lack of food, or probably a mixture of both, bring about another stab of light-headedness that consequently makes us queasy. It's a horrible feeling, a bit like seasickness, and it's just another pain I wish we didn't have to deal with on top of everything else.

***

The night is one of the longest I can remember. I wish I'd never read about the headless horseman because every sound has me imagining the cloaked figure and hearing his horse's hooves galloping toward us in the dark. Telling myself we don't have any cattle for him to steal, and therefore he should have no reason to bother us, only helps until the next rustle or snapping twig makes me jump again.

He doesn't come, of course. Two trucks pass, but both whisk by with better things to do than stop at a rest stop they probably can't even see in the dark. Unless they're *too afraid* to stop here.

Shortly after an anxiously awaited sunrise, I hear a third truck and notice a car a little way behind it, but both are heading in the wrong direction. When another car approaches from the north, I rush to wake Shadow so he can get to the road in time to show himself. He snaps to life a little too quickly for his empty stomach and dry mouth. The light-headedness comes on stronger than yesterday, and he's only on his feet for a second before the world around us spins and he is forced by the weight of his own body back to the ground.

The car is long gone by the time our heads clear, and although Shadow begs to go back to sleep, I'm too afraid that if he does, he might decide to stay that way. He's already lost a frightening amount of weight, so much that he's starting to remind me of the old, abandoned dog we once found. His head seems too bulky for his body now and the swelling that's blown his injured leg up like a balloon is making the other three look like knobby little sticks.

"It's time to get moving," I tell him, doing everything in my power to ignore his pleading eyes that have lost all of yesterday's determination. "We can't just sit here and wait to die."

Shadow limps beside me to the bitumen, where we stare down along the broken white line until it fades into a distant haze of blue sky and green grass.

"Astrid's only just down the road," I assure him, taking the first step of what will hopefully be our last stint. "We'll be there before you know it."

35

Visible

I'd lost count of the sunrises even before the rest stop, and I wouldn't have a clue how many it's been since.

The pangs of Shadow's hunger repeatedly squeeze my stomach, along with the unbelievable thirst, the infection I can feel spreading through his leg, and the rib cage too afraid to suck in anything more than shallow breaths. They give us no reprieve. We are both in a constant, light-headed daze where the daylight is just hours and hours of blinding glare and the night-time too dark to see through.

We stop more than we start. Sometimes I turn to see how Shadow is doing, only to realise he's no longer behind me, and find he's deliriously wandered away from the road and fainted somewhere in the grass. Other times I can't even find the road myself. It's there, beneath my feet one minute, and the next time I look down, I'm walking on dirt or lying in the middle of a paddock with cows all around.

I thought, by now, at least one car would've stopped to help. We've seen a few, I think. Maybe we haven't. Maybe they were just more delusions like the truck that pulled up, where Mick got out and ran to Shadow, or the faded, bottle-green ute that stalked us for an entire day, frightening us so much we stumbled as fast as we could into a nearby gully and hid, waiting to hear the voices of Greg and Sam that thankfully never came.

Eventually my stomach begins to feel like it's eating itself from the inside out. I can't remember when Shadow last ate, apart from the sausages he later threw up. I know it was before the rest stop. I remember looking away while he picked at a rotten pile of bones that may once have belonged to a kangaroo. I think that was even before the harvester, but I don't know anymore.

I wish I could look away again now. The starvation is well and truly showing in the sharp contours that jut from beneath Shadow's skin and in the coarseness of his once-silken coat. His paws are cracked and his nails are filed into blunt squares from the constant scraping on hard ground. Despite all of that, as well as a back leg that's seeping blood and pus, and is so swollen it won't bend anymore, he still follows me.

With every step his body weakens, and his once effortless stride is reduced to a series of laboured movements. Each time he faints, and I have to pick him back up, I tell him, "Just a little further."

I feel everything he does. All I want to do is stop and go to sleep and never wake up, but I can't. Not here. Not like this. I owe it to Shadow to keep moving, to fight harder than I think I ever could have in life. I owe it to Astrid as well, but more than anything right now, I owe it to Mick.

It feels like a lifetime ago that we met, and then lost him, but his memory still courses through Shadow's veins as though he will remain a part of him for as long as he lives. He was, without doubt, the highlight of our journey, the one beautiful person that both Shadow and I wish we could have held on to, and I know that If he hadn't have met Shadow and I, he'd most probably still be alive.

***

The sun sets, rises, and then sets again. The birds chirp, the moon shines and the stars twinkle. Critters crawl through the grass, kangaroos bound across the road, and we are oblivious to it all. There is no room left in my mind for anything outside of one simple thought – Keep moving, Shadow, just a little further – and I know this is all that lifts his feet.

***

At the dawning of yet another crystal-clear day, Shadow concedes defeat and stops.

I turn to urge him on, but his head hangs so low that his eyes can no longer rise to meet mine. His exhausted body shakes violently, and I know the wail of hunger rings so loud in his ears that he can't hear anything else – not even my pleading.

I watch him with agonising helplessness. There is absolutely nothing I can do to ease his pain. I can't carry him; I can't feed him. I am no longer his care giver, just an observer, and I alone have led him to this point of near-collapse. I have failed him when he trusted me the most.

When he finally gathers the strength to lift his head and lock his eyes onto mine, he does so with the dire yearning to hold them there for as long as he can; as though he's acutely aware that it might be for the last time. I see his resignation; his guilt for not being strong enough to continue. I see his heart so broken not even a thousand stitches could piece it back together. I can't, he is saying. I'm sorry, but I just can't go on.

I begin to cry. I cry for what could have been. I cry for Mick, and for a life with Astrid which Shadow may never know. "Please, Shadow," I beg. "You have to keep moving." But my words are wasted and Shadow's worn-out body drops to the ground.

I rush to his side. I lie down and press my ear to the sound of his hollow breathing. I run my hand along his body and am sickened by the way my fingers ripple over the sharp rise and fall of his ribs. I remember his once-gleaming coat and his eyes that would shine with so much life and vitality. I remember how he would nip at my heels when I was taking too long to get ready and how he would follow me with one of my shoes in his mouth, begging me to take him for a run. I remember how we would cuddle up together on the couch at night and how he insisted on staying so close to me when just a pup that he would actually stand in the shower with me. I remember our whole lives together, but those memories are now a thousand miles away and all but lost to the ominous calling of our desolate roadside graveyard.

My heart aches to no end, clouding my mind and cramping my muscles. I feel the tears escape my eyes and when I look down, I am astonished to see they are there, splashing on the ground, soaking into the bitumen, as real as if they had fallen from a living creature. I press the tip of my finger to the hard surface where one has landed, and when I remove it, there's an indent in my skin. A sharp prick jabs into my shoulder where it's squished under my weight against the ground. I lift onto my elbow to have a look, and see a tiny trickle of blood seeping out from where a shard of glass has pierced it.

This is so much more than the anger that drove me to be heard by John; these are real, physical feelings – and they're not Shadow's, they're my own. That's my blood!

The unmistakable sound of a car breaks the silence and immediately my heart begins to race. If I'm real enough to feel the road, real enough to bleed, then... am I real enough to be *seen*?

Heaving my now unimaginably weary body from Shadow's side, I force myself upright. The car draws nearer. A flash of red in the distance, traveling way too fast for anyone inside to notice an exhausted animal dying silently by the side of the road. I can't even be sure if it's real or just another delusion.

I have to believe. Whether it's real or not, I have to at least try.

I focus on its speed. I don't have the energy to exert myself for more than a second or two. If I try too early or too late, I might miss my chance.

It gets closer, closer.

As soon as I can see the outline of the driver behind the windscreen, I force my arms up as high as they'll go. They feel like cement as I crisscross them back and forth. I suck in a breath big enough to blow up a hundred balloons and use every last bit of my energy to cry out, "HELP US. PLEASE. WE'RE DYING!"

My voice pierces the cool morning air; as real as the

squawks from the birds that flee the trees above. The car whooshes past. It looks as though it's just going to drive on and I don't think there's a hole deep enough for my heart to sink into. It didn't work. Nobody saw me.

I don't know if I can bear to look at Shadow. How do I tell him that's it, we're done; it's all over? But when I finally do meet his eyes, I see they're not focused on me, they're focused on the road behind me, on the car – or more accurately, on the car's brake lights.

The driver must have had a delayed reaction, but they're definitely stopping, and as the car finally begins to pull over, I begin to fade.

My tears dry out, and as suddenly as it appeared, the touch of my skin is gone. The trickle of blood has vanished and the wound has healed. I open my mouth to cry out again, but my voice finds no volume, but it doesn't matter, because the car's doors have already swung open and the two people sprinting toward us have already seen Shadow.

"I'm certain of it," I hear the driver try to convince her male passenger, who overtakes her and drops to his knees beside Shadow. "There was a girl here. I saw her."

"There's no one around, Jen: see for yourself. Now help me get this dog into the car, would you? The poor thing's still alive."

36

News

The next time Shadow opens his eyes, it's from inside a cage.

The constant threat that has loomed over our heads since the beginning of our journey – don't get caught – jolts him to his feet, but four and a half days of sleeping have reduced his three good legs to jelly and left his injured one, with all its new stitches, opposingly tight. He wobbles dangerously and with a yelp, crashes back onto his severely bruised, but thankfully not broken ribs.

"It's ok, it's ok." I rush to calm him, wishing his first moment of consciousness could have been a less panic-inducing one. "You're safe, Shadow. We're not at the pound. We're at a vet. And guess what?"

Shadow's breathing gradually returns to normal. He blinks the sleep into the corners of his eyes and bends to briefly investigate his stitches, but the adrenalin and effort spent forces his eyelids back down to narrow slits. He stays awake just long enough to focus on me for the good news.

"We're in Deniliquin, Shadow. The vet they brought us

to, I heard her talking the other day about having to go into *Echuca* for something. We must be right near Astrid."

***

Another twenty-four hours slip by before Shadow wakes again. He's rested and fully alert when the vet comes to check on him, and for the first time since his almost lifeless body was thrust into her rolled pork arms, four days ago, the worried lines I thought were permanent fixtures on her face relax into a genuinely pleased smile.

She sounds like she's practicing for a role in a musical as she sings, "Well, good morning."

Possibly hoping for the part of the jolly mother, she opens Shadow's cage as though she's drawing musty drapes aside to let the sunshine in on a sleeping child. "My! My!" She tones the singing down to a chirp. "You are a tough little one. I didn't think you were going to make it there for a while."

Her dimpled hands reek of disinfectant as she runs them up and down Shadow's legs, feeling her way around his stitches and over every joint. "My! My!" She continues with a respectable amount of awe, "What a gash! Right down to the bone. You're lucky, you know. Left any longer, I would have had to take the whole leg off. Don't go sniffing at it now or I'll have to put a cone on your head."

Without so much as a wince, Shadow allows her gentle hands to do their job.

"How you're even alive, considering your condition." Her awe heightens. "I've seen more meat on a filleted fish. And given how far you've come..."

The statement stirs my curiosity. How does she know

how far we've come? But I could have saved myself the question, because deep down, I already know the dreaded answer, and without further ado, she confirms the worst. "I scanned your microchip."

A part of me wants to stay hopeful. We're so close to Astrid, Mum would have to be crazy not to let her take Shadow now. Surely she's not still mulling over their argument or stuck on the whole my daughter, my dog thing. But apparently she is, and the vet couldn't be more overjoyed to tell Shadow all about it. "I found your owner, Shadow." She purses her lips and sighs before the next part. "Well, your owner's mum, that is. I'm so sorry about what happened. How on earth you ended up all the way down here is beyond me, but guess what?" She takes a deep breath like she's ready to sing again. "You're going home. She's organising transport as we speak, and as soon as you're well enough to travel, you can go. Isn't that wonderful?"

I know she's only doing what she believes is right, but it doesn't stop me from screaming inside my head, 'NO! It's *not* wonderful. It's the *worst* possible thing that could happen!

As hard as I try, I can't keep the terrible image of Shadow returning to Claire bundled under wraps in my mind. It escapes and Shadow sees it. It sends him quivering back into the far corner of his cage.

The vet mistakes his retreat for fear of her touch. "Aww! Poor baby. You're still a bit sore, I know." She works her arms, one after the other, out of Shadow's cage and locks the door. "I'll come back a bit later and we'll see how well you can walk then, huh? Who knows, maybe I can give you the all clear in a couple of days. There's not much else we can do with your ribs or that leg except give them time to heal, and you'll have to be on a strict diet so you don't gorge yourself sick." She says it like she's trying to sway Shadow from an addiction. "Your insides have really taken a beating, you know. But," here comes the reward, "I know you probably *can't wait* to get home, and given how quick you seem to heal, you could be on your way as early as the day after tomorrow." She practically floats out of the room singing *Isn't It Wonderful*. If only she knew what this means for Shadow.

Left alone, Shadow and I can't bring ourselves to do more than stare at the floor in sullen silence. 'As soon as you're well enough to travel': those were the vet's words. 'As early as the day after tomorrow'. The thought not only makes me shudder, it also makes me feel – sick.

Sick! That's it! If Shadow doesn't get better, she won't send him.

37

No more delays

Five days later: Shadow's chronic limping, over-dramatic pained groaning, and refusal to eat while being watched is no longer fooling anyone.

If he could stop eating all together, we might be in for a better chance of staying, but after so long on the road without food, it's not something he can completely avoid. There's nothing but skin on his bones as it is, and I don't think either of us could go through the pain of starvation a second time.

We've tried everything to keep the vet from declaring him fit, but all her x-rays, scans and checks contradict Shadow's behaviour, and now the tomorrow morning we've done everything possible to put off has arrived. The animal transport van is here.

The sliver of hope that Astrid might come to rescue Shadow is a wasted effort. We've heard the vet on the phone to Mum on numerous occasions. Not once was there any mention of Astrid, or of Shadow going anywhere but north. If Astrid knew Shadow was here, she would have come. Nothing in the world could have stopped her.

Trying to find a way to escape has been an even bigger waste of time. Shadow's cage is constantly latched shut with a twist carabiner shackle. The vet must have had previous escapees to enforce such a dog-proof system. His fake chronic limping has also hindered any attempt. Because of it, the vet hasn't dared to take him walking further than a few tight-collared meters around the closed-door clinic's back room.

As hard as it is to fathom, we're heading back to Cairns. I guess from there, we'll just have to start our journey all over again.

***

I can hear the transport driver and the vet talking out in the clinic's reception. Old Keith, she's calling him, and he must be bordering on going deaf because the vet's had to repeat her request to make sure Shadow's kept comfortable three times already.

I've heard Keith ask her each time, "What's that?" He's doing it again now, prompting her to speak loud enough to be heard throughout the entire clinic. "No need to shout," he answers before promising to take the best care possible.

A moment later, the vet is at Shadow's cage with a brand-new collar and lead. She proudly shows Shadow the personalised name tag dangling beneath. "I had something made for you," she says, flipping the tag over. "See? It's the shape of Australia. And look here." She points to the east coast side. "I had them engrave a little dotted line to show how far you travelled."

It's such a sweet gesture from such a sweet woman, one who has cared for Shadow with so much heart that I know there's no way she would put him in the cargo van waiting outside, if only she knew his story – but she doesn't. And so, with a click, she closes the collar around Shadow's neck.

Shadow's no more prepared than I am to give up. He straight away lifts his injured leg and yelps as though it hurts too much to walk.

The vet knows better. "Oh, come on." She shuts him down. "I've checked that leg a thousand times already. It's healing beautifully, and with the number of painkillers you're on, I'm pretty certain you can't even feel it."

She lightly pulls the lead, gradually shifting Shadow's weight forward until he has to put the leg down. Without hesitation, he snatches a front paw up and yelps again, this time making the vet laugh. "You obviously don't know where you're going, do you?" She tugs on the lead again. "I bet you'd be *running* out of here if you did. Come on, I know you're fine to travel. Trust me, *I'd know* if you weren't."

Out of ideas, Shadow looks at me for help. I tell him to lie down. With a groan, he flops like a lead weight to the floor of his cage.

This only succeeds in making the vet laugh harder. "Oh, my goodness, you're a stubborn little thing. Why on earth would you want to stay cooped up in here?"

Realising Shadow's not budging, she starts to drag him toward her on his side. He reaches the front of the cage, rolls onto his belly, and spreads both front legs out to press them against either side of the door.

The vet finds his antics all very amusing. She tugs on the lead with one hand and tries to dislodge Shadow's persistent grip on the cage with her other.

She's still laughing when Keith sticks his head into the room and calls out, "Will you be much longer, love? I'd really like to get going soon." He sees her dilemma and in one fell swoop puts an end to our tactics. "Leave him in there if you want. We'll carry the whole cage out: shouldn't be too heavy with a couple of us."

The vet dries her eyes and agrees. The cage door is shut, locked, and on the count of three, heaved off the ground.

Shadow is carried through to reception with me following behind like a one-person funeral procession. At least that's how it feels. There's no escape, no more delays. Our hope is dead and on its way to be buried. Even the shrill ringing of the reception phone doesn't break the mournful atmosphere. Nor the way the receptionist answers the call like she's running a dusty outback pub, rather than a polished country centre clinic. "G'day, Deni vets?"

Her chatter is nothing more than annoying background noise. It follows us all the way to the front door and halfway outside before something she says reefs me back into the land of the living. "They're just taking him out now, doll. Who said you could have the dog?"

The vet hears it too and twists her head around questioningly. "Hold on a sec, Keith," she says as loud as possible without shouting. She grabs the receptionist's attention with a mimed "Who is it?"

The receptionist shoots her an uncertain maybe-just-wait shrug and returns her attention to the phone. "Aha!" she says. "I see. Yeh, he's literally being carried out as we speak. Nah, sorry, doll. Your friend's mum's the legal guardian now. Without her consent—— Nah, it can't come from her boyfriend, his name's not on the microchip. Yeh, look, honestly, how far away are you again? Echuca? Yeh, I wouldn't bother. He'll be gone before you get here. The driver's gotta leave, like, now. Yeh, you're welcome to, but he won't be here."

The look on the receptionist's face says she's been hung up on.

"What was that all about?" the vet immediately wants to know.

Keith almost tips Shadow's cage up taking an obvious glance at his watch.

Nobody seems certain about what to do, and all I can think is, *that was Astrid*. She's on her way here.

Shadow's curled in the corner of his cage like a frightened mouse. If he jumps around and makes carrying him difficult, they might put him down. It could buy us some time.

Without waiting to hear the receptionist's long-winded explanation of the phone call, I relay to Shadow what I've heard. My heroic image of Astrid driving like a mad woman, busting open the clinic's door and throwing herself over Shadow's cage brings him out of his corner and onto his feet. There's no more limping, no pained groaning, no yelping, just a completely healthy dog spinning around, barking, howling, and scratching at his cage wires in a desperate bid to get out.

Keith struggles for a second under the topsy-turvy weight, but it's obviously not his first time dealing with a difficult dog, and he proves it by locking his iron grip around the wires and pulling the cage in close to his chest to steady it.

The vet also packs a surprising amount of muscle under her end, but doubt has crept in, and for a moment it looks as though she might be about to put Shadow down. "I don't think he wants to go," she mumbles to herself.

Keith turns an ear toward her. "What's that?"

The second time she says it it's barely any louder, as though it's still more of an uncertain thought than a statement. "I don't think he wants to go."

"Of course it's not going to snow." Keith baulks at the suggestion. "We're not in The Alps."

The vet finally speaks loud and slow enough to be understood. "No! I said... I don't, think, he wants, *to go*."

"Who?"

"Shadow! This dog here!"

"Ah! Now I'm with you. Look," Keith seems more than prepared to offer his expert opinion, "I wouldn't go getting too involved. I see these sorts of family disputes all the time. You're better off letting them sort it out."

"True," the vet half-heartedly agrees. "I've just never had a dog so determined not to leave before. Maybe it's because of this girl."

Keith's goodwill gets the better of him. "I'll tell you what. I've got to take him; I've been paid already and it's not good for business if I don't, but if anything changes, I've got my phone on me. Just give me a ring. Just make sure you do it sooner rather than later. I'm taking the Newell Highway because I like to stop at that Ned Kelly Bakery at Jerilderie. Good pies there...," he trails off before bringing himself sternly back to the moment. "but after that, I'm not turning around or stopping again. Ok?"

"Yeh, ok," the vet concedes. "Alright then, I suppose we should get him in."

38

Is it her?

Shadow and his cage are slotted between a couple of proper transport crates and strapped tight to one of the cargo van's padded walls. He's the only animal here so far. If no more join us, it won't only be a long journey, but a lonely one too.

The vet waits outside while Keith runs through a load shift check. Halfway through, he trips over a folded stack of blankets, loses his balance and falls front first over them like a rag doll, cursing on his way down, "Stupid damn blankets!"

From one top pocket of his logo'd pet transport shirt, a pack of breath mints falls out. He's too busy yelling to hear them rattle to the floor, and too busy answering the vet's concerned, "Are you ok in there?" to notice what fell from his other pocket – his phone.

***

There are two windows in the cargo van's back doors. They're both half-covered with the transport company's logo, leaving the inside with next to no light, but between the paint work I can see enough to watch Deniliquin fade to a tiny speck in the distance.

From his allotted place, wedged like a sardine on the floor, Shadow can see only wire, walls, the stack of blankets Keith tripped over, and beside them, Keith's phone. It's rung three times already, each time lighting the screen up with the same caller ID – Deni Vet Clinic.

Every piece of my heart tells me the calls are to do with Astrid. Something must have changed. After it started ringing the first time, I told Shadow to bark, to howl, to make whatever noises he could to alert Keith, but with Keith's limited hearing abilities, Shadow's efforts have amounted to nothing.

The last sign we passed told us we're not far out of Jerilderie. We're almost at the point of no return and Shadow's becoming hoarse.

***

The phone's rung eight times now, one call immediately after another, each one sounding more urgent than the last despite the unchanging tone. I can't pry my eyes from the back windows where our chance of seeing Astrid again continues to slip further and further away.

Keith stays true to his 'I'll keep him comfortable' word, sticking to an overly cautious speed that's resulted in a build-up of frustrated travellers behind us. Some overtake at the first opportunity, others sit behind with their driver's tapping their steering wheels or throwing their arms up as if to say: Come on!

There's one a little further back, about five cars deep in the line-up. It's a white hatchback similar to my old car and whoever's inside must be in an awful hurry. They're flashing their headlights and I think I can hear them honking.

I see the car in front of them pull over to let them pass. They've got their hazard lights on now as well, prompting three more cars to move over until they're only one space behind us.

Beside the stack of blankets, Keith's phone continues to ring. I've lost count of how many times it's been. I've even started to tune out to Shadow's barking.

The driver in the car directly behind us doesn't look happy about being held up from in front and honked at from behind. I can see him shouting into his rear-view mirror and pointing through his windscreen. It looks like he's saying *I can't go any faster.*

He steers to the right to peek past our cargo van for an overtaking opportunity. As he does, I catch a glimpse of the hatchback's passenger. I see a girl with her head down, like she's looking at something in her hand. Her long, brown hair has fallen forward, and as the car in front moves back to the left, she sweeps one half of it aside to clamp a phone to her ear. I lose sight of her before I get to see her face, but as soon as Keith's phone starts to ring again, my heart starts to cartwheel.

Shadow feels my mood change and clamps his mouth shut. He almost presses his eyeball through the front of his cage, trying to see up and through the window, desperate to know what it is that's caught my attention.

"Listen!" I tell him. "Can you hear that horn?"

Shadow listens. He hears the horn beeping repeatedly behind us and sees the hopeful picture forming itself in my head. It freezes him like a player in a game of statues. One that won't even breathe before the music starts again.

He waits for me to tell him more. When I don't, he pushes me with a bark. He needs to know if the image I'm sending has a face in it, but until I'm one hundred percent sure, I can't give him an answer. He's not the only one who wants to know. Is it her?

The car behind us finds a gap in the oncoming traffic. It pulls out to overtake, revealing the passenger again. Her head's not down anymore and the hair that had fallen forward has now been tucked behind her ears. One rounded, cherub cheek is lit up by the phone in her hand and her grass-green eyes are practically burning holes through the back of the cargo van.

The driver slides into view. The worried lines on her face are so deep they threaten to fold in on themselves. She's slapping her beefy palm against the car's horn like it's a bongo drum and I can just about make out her shouted words: "Answer your phone, you deaf old coot."

Shadow barks again and follows it through with a drawn-out whimper. He's done waiting. He wants an answer now. Is it her!

I turn away from the window as our cargo van starts to slow. Keith must have finally realised what's going on.

"Shadow?" I say, barely able to keep my words steady. "You'll never guess who's behind us." But Shadow no longer needs to guess because my image has a face to it now.

He quits his barking and goes back to trying to see out the window. The back of the cargo van falls into silence, even more so as Keith finds a place to pull over and kills the engine.

I don't bother looking out anymore. I want to be right beside Shadow when those doors open. I want to feel everything he does when his cage is unlocked and he's scooped into the arms of the one person we've fought so hard to find.

We hear car doors opening and shutting, footsteps sprinting, and Keith outside. "Why didn't you just ring me?"

The vet sounds like she's just run a marathon. "We've been trying, Keith! Where's your bloody phone?"

"It's right...Oh!"

"Oh, for goodness sake, Keith. Ring it again, would you, dear? And Keith! Open those doors. That dog's not going anywhere."

Keith's cell phone rings for the last time. As it does, we hear more footsteps, a jingling of keys and the turning of the lock. The back doors are flung open, flooding the cargo van with light that temporarily blinds us. I see Keith's silhouette first. "Just let me——" he starts to say.

"Oh, get out of the road." The vet cuts him off with a shove. "I'm sure you're the last person he wants to see right now."

Two new silhouettes appear, one resembling a bowling ball with arms, the other thinner, but with those exact beautiful curves I spent so many years envying.

Shadow's eyes take longer to adjust, prompting him to ask me one more time, is it really her? But before I can say a word, the girl outside leans in and Shadow's answer is staring him right in the eyes.

The answer is yes, Shadow.

Yes, it's Astrid.

***

I never thought I'd find myself loving Mum's boyfriend, Robert, or more specifically, Robert's allergies, but as it turned out, they're the one thing that tipped the scales.

According to the vet, who explained everything to old Keith at the same time as Shadow was bounding out of his cage and into Astrid's arms, it wasn't Mum's jealous ways that Robert had put his foot down on. It wasn't even the indisputable fact that Shadow had travelled three thousand kilometres to find the person he wanted to be with. It was the allergies.

Claire had said no way to taking Shadow back, then Robert had told Mum it's him or the dog, and Mum had been forced to make a choice. Thankfully she made the right one: one that now has Shadow happily trailing Astrid and the vet back to the little white hatchback that's going to take him home.

Watching him leave fills my heart with bittersweet emotions. He is with Astrid. He is safe and everything we've been through has proven worthwhile. Only now, with this beginning of Shadow's new life, comes the ending of ours. I am no longer needed. There is nowhere left for me to lead.

"You're where you belong now," I say to him, glumly realising he's forgotten to say goodbye.

After having clung to my side throughout our entire journey, when the time has come for us to go our separate ways, he doesn't seem the least bit fazed. Maybe he's forgetting me already. He turns his head back and I wonder if he can still see me or if I'm already gone.

"Shadow? Can you hear me?"

Astrid opens the car door, and with the help of the vet, bends to lift Shadow inside.

I call out to him, "I'll miss you," wondering why, amid this joyous occasion, I don't feel the completion I thought I would.

As Shadow is carried onto the back seat, he turns his head one last time and our eyes meet. Why are you not following, he wants to know; I'm not home yet.

39

Home?

We've been with Astrid and her parents for almost three months now. The only physical reminder of our journey is the scar on Shadow's leg, but for some reason, mentally, he hasn't settled as well as I thought he would.

I expected him to slot right back in to where he, Astrid and I left off when we lived in Cairns. I thought he'd divide himself between the two of us like he used to: spend his days with me while she is at university and his nights cuddling up beside her on the couch. I thought he would feel at home here, but sadly, it feels more like he's just biding his time in some sort of foster care.

Tonight is no different. Shadow and I are outside at his new favourite spot between the front of the family's old Victorian-style farmhouse and the start of their long, gravel driveway. It's the only place with an unobstructed view through all four windows and also a clear line of sight out to the fence line bordering Echuca-Mitiamo road, which has strangely become an obsession for Shadow.

The evening air is close to freezing and growing colder by

the second. I'm certain there'll be another frost in the morning. As usual, it doesn't make any difference to Shadow. He curiously prefers to stay out here and watch the road, rather than retreat to the warmth inside.

In the paddock to our right, Astrid's heavily rugged new horse, Toby, hangs his docile head over the fence. Infatuated with Shadow, he's never far away, always following and watching longingly like a cow without a herd.

Above us, the Milky Way spreads itself across the crisp, black sky. It's close enough to touch - just like Mick once said. I wonder, like he did then about his dog, Luna: if he's up there now, one of the stars looking down on us.

Light pours from the windows behind us. It spreads itself over the house's colonial-style veranda and seeps down into the manicured garden beds below. Inside I can see Astrid, along with her mum and dad. They're washing, drying, and passing each other dishes to stack away after tonight's spaghetti Bolognese.

Like every other night, Astrid spends more time looking out at Shadow than anything else. She's tried so hard since we've been here to make his life perfect. She's bought him the best food and the softest beds, taken him jogging every morning as she promised she would, taken him along on her ride-outs with Toby, and loved him unconditionally. Although Shadow shows endless amounts of gratitude, it's as obvious to Astrid as it is to me that for him, something is missing.

I keep asking him what it is, but each time I do, I receive only an image of him waiting out on the road. What he's waiting for he either doesn't yet know himself, or won't show me. He's just waiting.

***

Winter passes, Spring blooms and Summer burns. Eventually Autumn returns to strip the trees of their leaves for the second time since our arrival. In all this time, Shadow's behaviour hasn't changed. He is still unsettled.

Astrid refuses to give up on him. He now has an entire basket of balls and toys. She started buying them for him after his obsession with the road stopped him from following her on her jogs and horse rides. He has five of the softest dog beds imaginable scattered throughout the house, and when none of them lured him in, she bought him a weatherproof one and placed it outside in his favourite waiting spot.

After a while, the constant sight of Shadow alone out in the yard got the better of her. She bought herself a picnic blanket and bright, battery-powered lamp, and started bringing her study books outside every evening.

I couldn't have asked for a better friend, or a better owner for Shadow. I just wish I knew what it is that's still keeping him from feeling complete.

***

It's an early April morning when Astrid greets Shadow out on his weatherproof bed with his lead swinging from her hand. "We're going to the vet," she says apologetically. "It's time for your annual vaccine. The good news is it's the same vet that saved you. Remember her, Shadow?"

Shadow wags his tail as though he couldn't be more overjoyed, not because he understands what Astrid is saying, but because the way she says it makes it sound like it's something he really wants to do.

It isn't long before we are sitting in an all-too-familiar

waiting room. The pub-voiced receptionist, together with the smell of disinfectant and a couple of empty cages, bring back mixed-emotion memories of our last time here.

The same vet from the year before comes rushing out to meet Shadow. "Hello, little man," she gushes. "Look at you. No more skin and bones. What a difference."

Shadow feels safe in the vet's presence. He just about licks the wrinkles off her face and then throws himself to the floor, where he lies waiting for his welcoming belly rub.

"He looks excellent," the vet praises Astrid. "He must be happy. He certainly looks healthy."

Astrid accepts the praise with reserve. "Healthy, yes," she agrees. "But happy I'm not so sure about. He's always by himself, like he doesn't know how not to be lonely. When his owner, Lucinda, was still around, he was different: happy and excitable all the time. He followed her - and me - around like..., well, like a *shadow* back then. He doesn't seem to want to know me now. How long do dogs grieve for?"

"Who knows, really? I guess it depends on how close they were to the person who's died."

"He was really close to Lucy. They were pretty much inseparable."

The vet gives Shadow a big hug. "Poor boy," she says before turning back to Astrid. "All I know is I'm glad you came along when you did. After everything you told me, I dread to think what would have happened if we hadn't have stopped him from going back up north."

She starts to lead Astrid and Shadow toward the examination room, but stops again. "Actually," she holds a finger up like she's just remembered something exciting, "that reminds me. Not long after you took him, a young man called from somewhere up that way: a truck driver. He was looking for a blue cattle dog like Shadow. He said the dog had travelled with him to the Gold Coast, but then he lost him. He seemed like such a lovely young man...," the vet trails off in thought, "except for the drug problem."

Astrid can't hide her curiosity. "Drug problem?"

"Well," the vet continues sympathetically, "he said he OD'd because his drink was spiked by a couple of German backpackers, but... Well, you know kids your age better than I do, if you know what I mean. Anyway, he said he woke up in hospital and the dog was gone, but the backpackers were there. They felt so bad that they came back and helped him search for the dog. Apparently they searched the entire Gold Coast, and then some lady whose daughter was psychic or something – I don't know, it's a pretty out there story – she pointed them in this direction. So they rang around down here until they eventually found me. Oh," she adds, before Astrid can get a word in, "it gets better! The guy said that while he was OD'ing – he doesn't remember the paramedics or the trip to the hospital – he remembers a girl touching him."

"What's so strange about that? Was she his girlfriend or something?"

"No. he said she was just there one minute, touching his heart, and then gone the next. He seemed to think that it was the only reason he survived, said it brought his heart back into rhythm, and that the paramedics had called it a phenomenon. It's the only thing he remembers."

"So, who was she?"

The vet answers quietly, "Well, to me it sounded like he meant she was a ghost."

I see a shiver prickle itself over Astrid's arms. She sucks in a sharp breath and then banishes her thoughts with a resigned sigh. "Sounds like the whole drug thing might be a bit more of a regular occurrence than a one off, if you ask me."

"Maybe, but it was still a great story. And he left his number in case Shadow ever needed a home again. Don't worry; I didn't pass on your details, of course."

There is not a breath in my lungs, but if there were, it would be caught. There has long since been a beating of my heart, but in this moment I imagine I can feel it pounding through my chest. I understand now what Shadow has been waiting for. Why he has felt so compelled to watch the road. I reach my hand down and let it fall to rest on his head. "It wasn't Mick we saw in that ambulance, Shadow. Mick is alive."

40

Listen!

I follow Astrid through the house, constantly whispering and pleading in her ear. Shadow stays at my heels and together we play an anxious game of waiting.

Since our visit to the vet over two weeks ago, I have spent my time fiercely attempting to push my way inside Astrid's thoughts.

Shadow plays his part as best he can. He senses the trucks long before they roll into sight and springs into a frenzy that often upsets Astrid and has her scolding him. To begin with, she appreciated Shadow's apparent change of mood and thought maybe he'd finally gotten over his grief. As time dragged and she found herself less willing to be constantly barked at, tugged on, and pounced all over, she began questioning why the sudden impish behaviour.

Now, as we glue ourselves to her every move, her aggravation grows and I wonder when she will begin to listen.

The weeks pass and another Winter slowly settles into the brick walls, and Astrid's face becomes a picture of constant frustration. Aside from the barking, tugging, and pouncing,

Shadow has found an array of irritating ways to alert her to the passing of each truck. He rips her blankets from the bed, sometimes in the dead of night, and drags them to the front door, where he scratches at the wood until it is carved with hysterical claw marks. He tears the pages from her study books as she attempts to read and even knocked the tv over once, almost smashing it, while her parents were out and she was trying to watch a movie.

He rips her washing off the line as she attempts to peg it down, then bolts off down the driveway, dragging wet clothes through the dust and all over the gravel until he reaches the boundary gate.

Here I watch him waiting, beckoning Astrid to follow him and see what he is so desperately trying to show her, but by the time she has cursed and stomped her way to the road, the trucks have already rolled by and Shadow's efforts are misunderstood and reprimanded.

"Mum and Dad won't let me keep you if you keep doing this, Shadow," she always warns.

On a particularly cold night, after the family have washed away the remains of a late tv dinner and snapped off all but one of the lights, Shadow and I follow Astrid to the front steps, where she wraps a blanket around her shoulders and takes a seat under the stars.

Shadow lays himself at her feet and fixes his focus on the end of the moonlit driveway.

I watch Astrid follow his stare with curiosity. "I don't understand you, Shadow," she says. "Are you trying to tell me something? Is that why you're always being so naughty these days?" The frustration that usually taints her voice has diminished somewhat and her question comes out weary and defeated. "I don't know what to do with you anymore. I promised I would look after you. I promised my parents you wouldn't be a problem and I'm trying as hard as I can, but..."

She turns to the sky for her next words, unsure if they should be spoken. "Mum and Dad have had enough. There isn't a sheet left in the house that isn't torn. The dining table and front door look like we've got a wild bear caged inside, and every day I go to university in clothes stained with dirty paw marks. I know you're miserable, Shadow. Is it still Lucy? Even after all this time? I want you to be happy. I really do. I want us all to be happy. I miss Lucy too, but maybe losing her was just too much for you."

When Astrid reaches down to Shadow, her guilt couldn't be more obvious if it were tattooed across her forehead. "I hate the idea of giving you up. I feel like it's the worst way I could possibly let Lucy down. But as Mum said, the idea of seeing you this miserable is way worse. Maybe being with me is making it too hard for you to get over Lucy."

As I lean into Astrid's ear to resume my harrowing pleading, I see Shadow raise his head and prick his ears.

"What is it?" Astrid asks, searching the empty driveway.

A distant rumble breaks the evening silence and brings Shadow to his feet. In an instant, he begins his usual tricks. He tugs and yanks at the corner of Astrid's blanket until the sound of tearing thread sees him stumbling backward. Clutching the strip of fleece between his teeth, he lets out a muffled bark and bounds down the steps, begging Astrid to follow him out into the night.

As the sound grows louder and more distinct, Astrid angrily jumps to her feet, pulls the rest of the blanket tighter around her shoulders, and stomps after Shadow. "Come back here," she demands. "Bring that back. Mum's going to freak."

Shadow stops on the grass to make sure Astrid is following, and when she catches up to him and makes a swipe for the blanket in his mouth, he darts to the side and dashes further down the driveway.

I stay beside Astrid as she hastily picks her woollen-socked feet over the stones. "Hurry up," I whisper all the while. "You're going to miss it."

The driveway is long, but the truck is still a little while away, so Shadow pushes on with his game of cat and mouse until finally, as two beams of light break the darkness and bounce off the trees, we are at the gate.

Shadow spits his strip of blanket out, and as Astrid bends to retrieve it, he jumps up and presses his paws to the gate.

"I don't get you," she lectures. "You make me chase you all the way down here and then you simply stop. For what, Shadow? I honestly don't understand."

The rattle of the engine draws nearer and Shadow begins to bark.

"What is it with you and these trucks?"

Shadow's barking turns to a mournful, almost painful howl. It's strung together by a yearning that can't be overheard, any more than the chill it sends up Astrid's spine can be overlooked. It leaves her shivering.

"You brought me here for something, didn't you?" She folds her arms across her chest and peers into the oncoming headlights. "I'm listening now," she whispers. "Please tell me what you are waiting for."

Shadow continues his howling and I increase my pleading. With the same desperation as once on the roadside, I push pictures into her mind: images of Shadow and Mick; visions of highways, truck stops, the Surfers Paradise Beach at night, and Shadow being driven away from the hospital.

Hypnotised by the blinding lights, together with the sudden barrage of thoughts, Astrid's face changes to reflect the sad story she's being told. Her eyelids flutter closed. Her breathing escalates. Her arms weaken until they flop to her sides, and as the truck slices through the air, leaving her blanket flapping to the ground, her hand rises to her mouth and a long-awaited look of realisation freezes her stare.

Long after the road is empty and the night is once again bathed in silence, Astrid drops to her knees and takes Shadow's head in her hands. "It wasn't just a story, was it?" she murmurs, as though the images still roll through her mind. "It was you – on the Gold Coast. And the girl next to the paramedics? Oh my God, Lucy!"

The following morning, Astrid reaches for the phone and I hear her ask a question that will forever silence my pleading. "You wouldn't still have the number of that truck driver, would you?"

41

He's coming

It is a sun-drenched Sunday afternoon, as quiet and ordinary as any other. I stand with Shadow behind our mesh-wire boundary and listen for anything that might disturb the silence. When I look behind me, and back down the driveway, I see Astrid. She's perched on the edge of the steps at the front of the house, and just as she did on the day of my wake, she watches Shadow.

I don't need to study her face to know it's no longer plagued with guilt, sorrow, or frustration. I don't need to read her thoughts to know she no longer worries for the emptiness in Shadow's heart. Her smile is one of conclusion. She knows she has found the one piece of his puzzle that has been missing for over a year.

When I turn back to Shadow, I catch his gaze, and once again see the same vision he had showed me, over and over, since the very first day of our journey: Astrid, Mick, the quiet country road, the feeling of euphoria.

I told you, says the satisfaction written all over his face.

"You did." I can't deny it. "You did indeed."

His body is a picture of health and his eyes, that have so often portrayed the fear of defeat, now sparkle with renewed life. His ears prick to every movement in the grass, but it is the end of our bitumen horizon that holds his focus. He is waiting, as he has done every day, for a distant rumble and a flicker of silver light.

High over our heads, the wind rustles through the trees. It sounds like a murmur of voices, and when I listen closely, it's almost as if I can hear distinct words: he's coming!

The wind picks up and lifts the silver-studded hairs on Shadow's back. I can feel the change in the air, as though nature itself has come to witness this final chapter of Shadow's tale.

A familiar sound touches my ears. It's faint, but distinct. A rumble, as quiet as a whisper, but loud enough to send Shadow's feet into a frenzy across the stones.

Far in the distance, where the tall grass seems to swallow the tar, I spot a glimmer of reflected light. The sun filters down through the trees and catches the tips of two exhaust stacks pointing high toward the sky and twinkling as though dusted in glitter. Two puffs of black smoke dissipate in the air and I know, beneath the swirling fumes, a caramel-headed, checked-shirt-wearing, beautiful, hazel-eyed man is pushing the turning of twenty-two wheels to their limit.

Shadow takes to the fence line, racing up and down on a celebratory high. When I glance behind me, I see Astrid rushing breathlessly up the driveway while her parents run out of the house to wait on the front steps, all of them asking, "Is it him?"

When Astrid reaches the gate, she leans over the wire and

sets her stare. Her eyes shine and her smile broadens to one of victory and relief. "Oh, Shadow. You're almost home."

The rumble grows louder and soon the truck, as black as night, with a front grill that looks like a furnace and a windscreen that looks like eyes, looms over the road. I remember being so afraid of it once upon a time. Now all I can see in it is a haven of safety and love.

Shadow's eyes dart from Astrid's to mine and back toward the road. His feet resume their dance of jubilation. I can hear his heart pounding and I can see the thoughts that fill his mind: he's here, he's really here.

It's almost upon us now, closing in with the crunch of a downward-changing gear and a sudden squealing of heated brakes.

Astrid unlatches the gate and hurries to the roadside. She throws her arms up and cries out through tears she can't restrain. "We're here!"

Shadow squeezes through the gate and scurries to Astrid's side. Unable to keep himself under control, he leaps, spins, and barks his long-overdue welcome.

The slowing truck roars by, flattening Shadow's ears and sending a haze of dust to sprinkle over his coat before eventually squealing to an idle.

Without a second to lose, Shadow sprints ahead to the truck's cab, where he waits, trembling with impatience, beneath the driver's side door.

With a squeak of un-oiled hinges, the door swings open, and as the first of two thonged feet stretches into sight, Shadow takes an almighty leap. Two sun-browned arms reach out and catch Shadow mid-flight. The momentum is enough to send both man and dog toppling back into the cab, and as Astrid buzzes in to get her first glimpse of the long-awaited stranger, I hear the most precious of sounds – Mick's heart-warming, glorious laugh.

Fighting to speak through an uncontrollably quivering bottom lip, Astrid calls up over Mick's legs, "I think someone's waited a long time to see you."

"He's not the only one." Mick sounds no less emotional. "After I lost him on the Gold Coast, I thought that was it. I never dreamed I'd find him again. When I got your phone call…well, I honestly can't tell you what it meant."

Securing Shadow under one strong arm, Mick carefully climbs from the cab. At the bottom, he gently places Shadow on the ground, lifts his head, and for the first time lays eyes on Astrid. I don't know who beams the brightest, but without a second thought, Mick closes the gap between them and pulls her into his arms like a long-lost love.

Sublimely overcome by the warmth and gratitude of a complete stranger, Astrid returns every inch of the embrace, and for a moment, the sun shines brighter and the world has shifted itself into perfect order.

I look down at Shadow, who sits himself proudly between the two pairs of feet, and when he glances my way, his broad grin reflects exactly what I'm feeling. "We did it!" This is a good home, a kind home where he will be loved and cared for better than anywhere else, but something *was* missing.

I remember Mick's words as we sat together in the cool night air at a deserted truck stop: who am I to dream? And I know that on this most magnificent of Sunday afternoons on the side of a quiet country road, with Shadow adoringly gazing up at him and Astrid holding him like she never wants to let go, Mick has been shown that he's not only worthy of dreaming, but of being someone else's dream too.

When Astrid does finally let go, she immediately fires off the one question she's been dying to ask: "Please tell me about the girl. The one you saw while you were...the one with the paramedics. What did she look like?"

Mick clutches his hands together to keep a tremble at bay. His smile disappears and he stumbles over his words. "I'd, ah...I'd seen her...before that. Before she was there that night, I mean."

Astrid's face mimics my lack of comprehension. When?

Flipping back through our time together, the only thing I can think of is when he reached out to me as we sat on the beach, but he'd dismissed the idea. He didn't see me.

His next words leave me even more baffled. "I saw her before she was...dead."

"You can't have!" I blurt, heard only by Shadow. I don't have any clear memories of Mick from my life, and if we knew each other well enough for him to know *my* face, wouldn't I remember *his*? The only thing I do remember is thinking how familiar his voice was. I remember thinking I'd heard it before, but then I thought that was just because the way he spoke reminded me of his mum, Rosie. That's all I could put it down to, since I'd never really met or known any truck drivers except for...except...oh my God!

The voice! It's the same one Shadow spoke to me in...the same one from outside my car window.

Mick is...my truck driver.

42

I guess it's goodbye

Mick confirms his part in my accident. It's a confession that falls out of his mouth like a waterfall, where one sorry word cascades down on top of another without rest.

Astrid hears all about how he'd found Shadow, about Shadow visiting his parents first, and about his most recent discovery; his mum knew all along about me. He tells Astrid the Nico and Mila story: their disappearance and guilty return to the hospital, and about how they helped him search for Shadow.

By the time Mick's waterfall runs dry, Astrid is not the only one left speechless by such an intricate and unfathomable story. I now understand George's reservations about telling Mick, so soon after my death, that the dog he'd found was accompanied by an angel. I understand Mick's boss's concerned tone; Mick's self-scorn after he tried to touch me on the beach; why he was so taken aback by my look-a-like at the truck stop, and why he didn't think he deserved to dream. I thought it was all because of the loss of the family farm. But it wasn't. It was all because of me.

Mick's noticeably shaken as his confession leaves him catching his breath. He draws a nervous circle in the dust with his foot, like he has more to say, but can't decide whether or not to say it.

"What?" Astrid asks, desperate to hear everything she can.

"The day of the accident..." Mick pushes through the nerves. "The girl...Lucinda...she said something else that made no sense at all, until a while ago – until I spoke to the Deni vet actually. She was obviously delirious. She was looking straight at me, but I don't know if it was *me* she was seeing, if that makes sense."

"What did she say?" Astrid needs to know.

"She said, 'You need to go to Astrid!'"

So I did say it out loud, but Shadow didn't hear me. Mick did!

The image of a little girl with wild, ginger curls springs to mind. Olivia. Her words crash through my ears and ring truer than I ever thought possible. 'I think the naughty people stay here, until the ones they hurt, don't hurt anymore.'

When she said it, I remember thinking only of Shadow, thinking he was the only one I was supposed to stay here for. But now it seems more and more like Rosie was right. It wasn't a coincidence that we met Mick. Everything fell into place, just as it needed to for me to make his life right again also. I guess I was never just *Shadow's* angel.

Astrid doesn't know what to say, any more than she knows what to think. Both hands are covering her mouth and her eyes are so red and watery that I don't know how she can see through the blur. She stays like this, in shocked silence, until Mick worriedly asks, "Are you ok?"

Astrid nods, sending tears dripping down her cheeks. "It's just..." she finally uncovers her mouth, "Lucinda...Lucy. She was my best friend. I...just...I...it's..."

"A lot to take in?" Mick helps her finish. "I know she was your friend." He admits. "The Deni vet told me a little about Shadow's story. I'm so sorry."

After a moment of silence, Astrid starts biting her bottom lip. "Do you think..." She then dares. "If that little girl saw Lucy, and you saw her too, do you think she might still be...here?"

"I am!" I answer, but as usual, Shadow is the only one who hears me.

He looks up at me, at first gleaming with pride, contentment, and the belief that life couldn't be more perfect than it is in this moment, but then his eyes narrow, as if confused by something.

"What is it?" I ask.

I reach down to stroke him, but his hair doesn't feel right. It's not soft like it should be. It's...tingly, like pins and needles. The same as it felt when I first came out of the nothing. It's a feeling that's both welcome and unwelcome. It's one I've known all along would return, and one that tells me Shadow is finally where he's supposed to be, but it's still one I could never quite prepare for. It means my time with Shadow is over.

Shadow's eyes begin to dart through the empty air. Where are you? they ask. Why can't I see you anymore?

I feel the pins and needles intensify until they eventually

take over my whole body, as though I'm disintegrating into a million pieces. The same calm I felt after my accident washes over me. There's no sadness, only a sense of fulfilment. I've atoned for my mistake. I've set things right again and the only thing left to say is, "I guess it's goodbye."

As my words slip out, they're so faint, they almost get carried away in the breeze. I don't know if Shadow hears them, but he lifts his nose, draws in the last whispers of my scent, and then closes his eyes, as though trying to hold onto a memory that's already begun to fade.

"You're home now," I say, feeling myself being swept up and away from Shadow.

"But I promise you, I will always be your angel."

43

Where's your angel?

It's been over a year since I left Shadow with Mick and Astrid. As promised, I still watch over him, but I do it from afar now: unseen, unheard and unfelt. I can't lie; it took a little while to get used to no longer being missed or needed, but it doesn't matter, and I don't even mind, because it's not my story anymore. It's Shadow's, Mick's and Astrid's story now, and it's a beautiful one.

Shadow stayed with Astrid and her parents to start, but he wasn't alone. Mick was welcomed with open arms by all and didn't end up driving away again for a whole week.

When he did eventually have to go back to work, Shadow was right there beside him like a king on a throne. Only this time, Shadow's throne was in between the two front seats, between Mick and his new navigator, Astrid.

Together the trio drove all the way up to Babinda to pay someone a surprise visit: three people, to be more precise.

Claire was the first. When she opened the door, the guilt on her face made up for every terrifying moment Shadow and I had endured. She couldn't stutter through her apologies quick enough. Especially once Astrid told her the part about me *hanging around.*

Greg and Sam were next. Their visit didn't just come from Astrid, Shadow and Mick, it also came from the good people down at the local animal welfare association, followed closely by the police and two shiny pairs of handcuffs to replace their illegal guns and backyard kangaroo-shooting operation.

After that, Astrid returned to university. Mick's boss allowed him to change his route so he could visit Astrid every other week and Shadow patiently divided himself between the two for a while.

Then came the house, a simple beach-to-bush block Mick had been saving a deposit for. One nestled in the same tiny little town he had passed so many times on the highway and always hoped to one day live in – Cape Point.

Astrid finally finished university, and with the blessing of her parents, packed Shadow and her horse Toby up and moved in with Mick. A week later they bought a second horse and Mick finally got to take his long-awaited ride along the beach with the girl of his dreams. Of course, the speed of the ride was determined by Astrid's horse, Toby who, still infatuated with Shadow, wouldn't take one step ahead of him.

Mila and Nico kept in touch, even dropped in a couple of times before flying back to Germany. On one of those occasions, they got to meet Rosie and George too. I expected George to unleash hell on the two of them for what they did to Mick, but instead he handed them each a paintbrush and put them to work for the day restoring the old caravan Mick had found as a 40th wedding anniversary present.

While the restorations were taking place, Rosie snuck down to the beach with Shadow and the once abandoned Lab, Bobby, who'd turned out fatter and shinier than the Queen's favourite pooch. I watched Shadow and Bobby splash around in the water, roll in the sand, and eventually return to sun-bake contentedly by Rosie's side.

It was a perfect blue summer day without a cloud in the sky and just enough breeze to keep the heat at bay. Rosie watched Shadow with the same expectation as she had done during our very first visit. She knew all about me by this time and she was obviously still in awe of all that had happened.

I saw her reach down and cup Shadow's head in her hands. She looked deep into his eyes, just as she had done before, wondering if I was still around, and asked him, "Where's your angel now then?"

The question pricked Shadow's ears. He tilted his head toward the golden rays of sunlight that danced across the ocean. He lifted his nose to the breeze that swept across the sand and swirled into the sky. He got to his feet and turned away from the beach as though searching, and when his eyes finally came to rest on Mick and Astrid up on the property, he turned back to Rosie and bestowed her with his huge blue heeler smile.

'They're right there. Can't you see them?'

The end

About the Author

Among other things, Leesa Ellen is a truck driver, heavy machinery operator, creative photographer, former horse trainer, and author.

She spent many of her early adult years living in America and then Germany, before returning to her home country, Australia, where she now resides on the central Queensland coast with her two dogs and two cats.

Shadow's Angel is her first title to be released.

CPSIA information can be obtained
at www.ICGtesting.com
Printed in the USA
LVHW080503200721
693073LV00010B/1058